LABOR RELATIONS

LABOR RELATIONS

•

Georgie Lee

AVALON BOOKS
NEW YORK

Published by Avalon Books,
an imprint of Thomas Bouregy & Co., Inc.
160 Madison Avenue, New York, NY 10016

Library of Congress Cataloging-in-Publication Data

Lee, Georgie, 1974–
    Labor relations / Georgie Lee.
        p. cm.
    ISBN 978-0-8034-7712-4
    1. Women lawyers—Fiction.   2. Industrial relations—Fiction.
3. Motion pictures—Production and direction—Fiction.   I. Title.
    PS3612.E2245L33 2011
    813'.6—dc22

                                                    2010031066

PRINTED IN THE UNITED STATES OF AMERICA
ON ACID-FREE PAPER
BY HADDON CRAFTSMEN, BLOOMSBURG, PENNSYLVANIA

Acknowledgments

Special thanks to Terri Kauffman for her insight and honest opinions, and to all my friends in Los Angeles who helped me turn my entertainment industry experiences into a memorable story.

Chapter One

Sarah Steele's stomach tightened as the number flashed across the phone's caller ID screen. Jake Rappaport, the head of Labor Relations at Lion Studios, the most feared labor relations attorney in Hollywood, was on hold.

"I hear Rappaport is on your line."

Sarah looked up to see her co-worker Rachel standing at the door of her office.

"Why do you think he's calling?" she asked, knowing enough about Lion Studios' tactics to be nervous.

"To yell." Rachel shot her a sympathetic look, then walked off.

The light continued to blink, forcing Sarah to shake off her fear. She'd faced down angry lawyers, fiery judges, and irate slumlords. A studio labor relations attorney would be a walk in the park.

Slipping on her headset, she punched the button. "Sarah Steele. How may I help you?"

"Sarah Steele, you must be new." The deep voice slid out of the phone, masculine, smooth, the kind to narrate a summer blockbuster or make a woman's toes curl. At least if he was going to scream, he was going to do it in a voice to make a girl melt.

"Yes, I am."

"Congratulations. I'm calling about the demand for *Tidal Wave*."

Sarah sifted through the mountain of files on her desk, unable to believe the mess the previous attorney had left. The piles were completely unorganized, covering the desk, the filing cabinet, and the floor along one wall. She had no idea where the *Tidal Wave* file was or what the claim involved. She thought about putting Jake Rappaport on hold, but something in the confident tone of his voice told her he wouldn't wait for her to prepare. Instead, she let him keep talking while she dug through the files.

"Of course we dispute everything in the claim," he continued.

"Of course," Sarah agreed, struggling to catch the files sliding off the desk.

"Saucy too. I like that in an attorney." He chuckled, much to her regret. This was no way to start a professional relationship.

"Listen," he continued, "I like to meet the new attorneys. What do you say? Tomorrow? The commissary here at Lion Studios, one o'clock?"

"I'll have to check my schedule," Sarah stalled, tearing through a pile on the floor and finding the *Tidal Wave* file buried at the bottom. Tossing it onto her desk, she flipped furiously through it for a copy of the arbitration demand.

"Great, I'll see you tomorrow at one." The line went dead.

"It was a pleasure meeting you too," Sarah replied sarcastically to the silence, tossing her headset onto the desk. Glancing out her office door, she studied the large movie poster over the secretary's workstation. It was for a classic film she had never seen. Everyone else at the Movie Actors Guild had probably seen it a dozen times and could quote every line of the script. People in Hollywood loved to quote movie lines; it was practically a requirement for residency. Movies weren't Sarah's thing, and she couldn't quote a line from one to save her life. So what was she doing working as in-house counsel in the legal department of an actors' union?

She whirled around in her chair, studying the great view of Hollywood from her office window. A thick haze covered the famous Hollywood sign standing on the hill behind the Griffith Observatory. Both landmarks silently overlooked the numerous buildings, billboards, and trees filling the space between there and the MAG building on Wilshire Boulevard. The first few days after starting at MAG she'd marveled at the view. Now, the piles of demands for unresolved violations of a lengthy Codified Basic Agreement she barely understood dulled a bit of the Tinseltown glitter.

"I guess I'd better start learning," she said to herself, turning back to her desk and flipping through the *Tidal Wave* documents. After all, wouldn't her ex-fiancé, David, just love to see her crawl back to Richmond in shame? She wouldn't give him the satisfaction.

"What did Rappaport want?" a female voice asked.

Sarah looked up to see her boss, Bonnie Weston, standing in the doorway. Like almost all Los Angeles women, she was tall, thin, and dressed in the latest fashion: a tight skirt with a flare at the bottom paired with a crisp white shirt and three-inch high heels. Despite MAG's business casual dress policy, which Sarah heartily embraced in her black slacks and button-down shirt, everyone else looked as if they'd stepped from the pages of a fashion magazine. She'd never before worked with such a stylish group of liberal lawyers and labor workers.

"He called to discuss the *Tidal Wave* demand," Sarah replied.

Bonnie arched one perfectly tweezed eyebrow. "Did he yell?"

"No, he invited me to lunch."

"That's a new one." Bonnie looked surprised. "He must like you. Maybe you can tame the savage beast."

"I've never lunched with a rival attorney before. Should I go?" The whole idea seemed strange.

"Sure, everyone does. It's a great time to discuss claims."

"What exactly is the claim?" Sarah hated to ask, but she didn't have a choice. Having worked for a union before, she knew that union members had the right to file claims against employers who violated the provisions of a negotiated Basic Agreement. Usually the claims were limited to issues of pay or overtime. However, MAG provisions were pretty unique to the entertainment industry and dealt with everything from residuals to dressing rooms. Actors were constantly filing claims against producers for violating one Basic Agreement provision or another, and when the business representatives couldn't resolve a claim, the file landed on an attorney's desk. Most of the time the attorneys could negotiate a settlement, but when they couldn't, the file went to arbitration.

"It's a big one. Lion Studios is using some obscure language in the residuals provision to avoid paying the full residuals percentage on basic cable reruns. We have no choice but to arbitrate."

"Residuals provision?" With only a few days of training on the Basic Agreement, Sarah still found the majority of its provisions baffling. Although she had a vague understanding of how residuals worked, she didn't yet know enough details to argue a case.

"Section A(10). Producers pay residuals when a TV show reruns or a theatrical film plays on network TV. But when they sell a TV show or movie to a cable TV outlet, they pay residuals based on a percentage of the contracted sale price. Lion Studios is trying to undercut the percentage they're required to pay. Call the residuals department and have someone down there explain it. I need you up to speed fast. If MAG loses this arbitration, it'll set a precedent for the other studios to follow. Actors could lose millions of dollars in residuals."

Sarah fought back her rising panic. "Are you sure I should be handling this? I've only been here a couple of weeks. I hardly know the Basic Agreement."

"You can do it." Bonnie smiled with more confidence than Sarah felt. "Anyone who took on Taylor Manufacturing can handle Lion Studios."

Bonnie walked off, leaving Sarah more worried than before. If everyone knew the truth about her victory over Taylor Manufacturing on behalf of the workers' union, they wouldn't trust her with a car accident claim, much less a major union arbitration. Sarah looked at the poster, wondering again if she'd made the right decision. It didn't matter now. Picking up the phone, she dialed the residuals department and made an appointment to meet with the manager to go over the basic cable provisions. No matter what happened, she had a job to do at MAG, and she planned to stick with it, especially if it proved David wrong.

With a sigh of relief, Sarah turned the car off Wilshire Boulevard into her quiet neighborhood. After two weeks she still wasn't used to the frantic level of LA traffic, and maneuvering her Nissan Sentra through the demolition derby of BMWs and Mercedes didn't exactly help her relax after a long day of arguing with producers. Loosening her tight grip on the steering wheel, she drove slowly down the apartment-lined streets. She hated her commute, but she enjoyed the neighborhood her roommate, Dinah, affectionately called "the slums of Brentwood." In its numerous apartments and condos, studio assistants lived next door to midlevel managers, while a few old Hollywood stars called the more expensive buildings home. Despite the strange demographic, the neighborhood sported well-manicured front lawns, updated buildings, and a number of coffee shops, restaurants, grocery stores, and bookshops all within walking distance. The mix gave the area a hip but not too trendy vibe Sarah loved.

Pulling into the parking structure beneath the condo complex, she grabbed her stuff and headed up the short flight of steps to the front of the Spanish revival–style building. Punching in her security code at the wrought iron gate, she strolled through the complex's courtyard, stopping to dip her hand into the pool. Small waves danced on the steamy surface, distorting the underwater light. A puddle and wet footprints led toward one of the other condos, betraying the pool's recent use. Sarah smiled, knowing she'd never have gone swimming outside at the end of November when she lived in Richmond. With her parents and friends enjoying record low temperatures back home, she looked forward to indulging in this LA habit and made a mental note to find her bathing suit and take a dip.

"There you are. I've been waiting for you," a familiar voice called out as Sarah climbed the stairs to the second level. Dinah leaned against the open doorway of the condo, looking every inch the California girl despite her Virginia roots. Her blond hair fell about her shoulders, covering the top of the baby-tee she'd paired with dark skinny jeans to highlight her yoga-toned body. They'd been best friends since high school, remaining close through all the separations of college and life. Dinah had helped her get the job at MAG, then jumped at the chance to make Sarah her roommate, an offer Sarah couldn't turn down.

"Do you want to walk up to Brentwood Café for dinner?" Dinah asked as Sarah slipped past her into the shabby-chic living room.

"Sounds better than the frozen dinner I'd planned." Sarah quickly changed into a pair of jeans and a light sweater. Within minutes they were walking up the street toward the Brentwood Café, Dinah venting about her harrowing day as a publicist at Lion Studios.

"So the star sets up a meeting so he can thank us for all our hard work. Afterward, he has the nerve to complain about needing to take some time off because he's been working steadily for the last two years. Boo-hoo. Why doesn't *he* try getting up every day and working for people like him?"

"If I didn't know you, I'd think you were making this up." Sarah giggled.

"Don't laugh yet. Working with actors, it won't be long before you pick up a few war stories of your own," Dinah warned with a knowing look.

"I have the sinking feeling you're right."

They continued up the street toward tree-lined San Vincente Boulevard, passing joggers and other walkers out enjoying the warm evening. Brentwood Café sat on the corner of San Vincente and Barrington Boulevard, offering a prime view of everyone making their way to the shops and restaurants from the nearby neighborhood. According to Dinah, if Sarah wanted to spot a star strolling down the street drinking a double latte, this was the place to do it.

"There's a table by the window. Quick, snag it." Dinah pushed Sarah into the restaurant, then rushed past her and slid into the small booth before a couple hurrying in from the other side could claim it.

Offering the couple an apologetic smile, Sarah sat down across from Dinah. "I still can't get used to the competition in this city."

"Yeah, it's kind of weird, but when in Rome . . ." Dinah shrugged, handing her a menu from the stack behind the napkin dispenser. "Speaking of competition, is MAG still everything you hoped it would be?"

Sarah flipped open her menu with a sigh. "It's a job, and it's not in Richmond. It's still everything I hoped it would be."

"Come on, Richmond wasn't so bad."

"Not Richmond. David."

"Oh." Dinah nodded with a sympathetic look. Having spent hours on the phone listening to Sarah cry after David cheated on her, Dinah knew the whole sad story. "Have you heard anything from him?"

"No, but Lisa e-mailed me today. He already has a girl-friend."

"How kind of her to tell you," Dinah replied sarcasti-cally, sitting back while the server placed two waters and a basket of bread on the table.

Sarah closed the menu, more irritated than upset. "I don't want him back, and I'm definitely not jealous, but I want to know how the creep can find someone, yet I'm still single."

"His girlfriend is probably desperate," Dinah suggested. "Forget him."

"I already have."

"Good. Now we can concentrate on finding you a rich, handsome, successful boyfriend to tell Lisa about so she'll tell David."

Sarah shook her head. "I'm having enough trouble navi-gating the streets of Hollywood without getting sideswiped. The last thing I need right now is a relationship."

"Who said anything about a relationship?" Dinah laughed, then leaned forward, a wicked look in her eye. "How about just a little arm candy? Someone to talk about when you go home to visit?"

"You mean lie about?"

"No one has to know the truth."

"The truth always comes out. Besides, I don't want the headache. All I want is to settle into my job and enjoy a nice, quiet, hassle-free holiday season."

Dinah cocked a suggestive eyebrow, signaling she heard

Sarah but refused to believe her. Luckily the waiter appeared, saving Sarah from having to explain her desire to stay single.

"Speaking of men," Sarah began after the waiter took their orders and left. "I'm having lunch with someone at Lion Studios tomorrow. Jake Rappaport."

Dinah stopped midbite of bread, her eyes wide. "You're kidding!"

"You've heard of him?"

"There isn't a woman at Lion Studios who hasn't heard of him. He's the hottest, most available bachelor on the lot." She pointed a well-manicured finger at Sarah, her look suddenly serious. "If you could engineer it for David to see you with a man, Jake would be the man."

"I can't date an attorney from the other side. It's a major ethics violation."

"I'm not talking about dating him. Rappaport likes starlets, lots of starlets. Not exactly long-term relationship material. Plus, he's arrogant." Dinah drummed her fingers on the table, her gaze wandering thoughtfully up to the ceiling. "I'm talking about taking a picture with your cell phone, then strategically e-mailing it to Lisa."

"As much as I'd pay to see David's face when he opened that e-mail, taking camera-phone pictures during a business lunch won't help me earn the other side's respect. Besides, David knows enough of the truth. He knows I'm here in LA working for MAG, while he's still in Richmond chasing ambulances. For now, that's enough."

Chapter Two

Sarah pulled to a stop in front of Lion Studios, a thrill of excitement coursing through her. Up ahead stood the famous Lion Studios gates, an icon even a film novice could recognize. They featured prominently in the opening of every Lion Studios film ever made, and seeing them in person gave Sarah a little taste of Hollywood's magic. Despite the traffic, the smog, and all the wannabe producers, this city could easily give her tingles.

She pulled up to the security booth, and a handsome young guard stepped out to greet her.

"Good afternoon," he said with a wink, offering her a silver-screen smile. Sarah resisted the urge to chuckle, amazed again at how even the security guards in LA possessed movie-star looks.

He handed her a parking pass and directions before waving her through the gate. She drove slowly on the studio streets, trying not to hit golf carts and extras as she headed toward the tall brown stone-and-glass office building dominating the far side of the lot. After pulling into the last available visitor's parking spot, she reapplied her lip gloss, gathered up her purse and briefcase, and made her way inside.

The building's interior matched the impressive exterior, with a wide atrium surrounded by multiple levels of offices. Walking past a coffee cart and numerous posters of Lion Studios' latest releases, she asked another handsome guard for directions, then took the glass elevator to the top floor.

The elevator doors opened directly into the Labor Relations office, and Sarah stepped forward, immediately noticing its masculine, modern feel. Like the building, this suite existed to remind meager unions and workers exactly where they stood in the scheme of Lion Studios' priorities. Black leather sofas, marble tables, and dark wood trim announced the commanding power of the men who worked here. The only feminine element was the very young assistant sitting behind the dark wood desk sorting mail. Despite the professional nature of her attire, her statuesque figure was well displayed by a trendy blazer and the tight shirt underneath. Sarah struggled not to sigh, wondering how an average woman could compete in a city full of such assets.

"May I help you?" the receptionist asked, sweeping Sarah's black skirt suit with a condescending gaze.

"Sarah Steele to see Jake Rappaport," she replied, pinning the girl with a hard, authoritative stare, refusing to be cowed by an assistant.

"Just a moment," the receptionist mumbled, quickly looking down to pick up the phone and announce Sarah to the muffled voice on the other end.

"Please be seated," she said, her voice a little friendlier. "He'll be with you in just a moment."

Sarah sat down on the edge of the large couch, wincing at the way the squeaking leather emphasized the eerie silence. Only the occasional ring of a phone or the click of a keyboard from one of the attached offices punctuated the extreme quiet. The lack of noise made it impossible for her to ignore the pantyhose biting into the backs of her legs. She hoped the snag on her upper thigh didn't run, then wondered again why she'd even bothered to wear them. No one else in LA seemed to worry about covering up.

"Sarah Steele, pleased to meet you." Jake Rappaport strode out of his office, a friendly smile on his handsome face. He wore his wavy brown hair combed back, emphasizing his strong nose and square jaw. A light button-down shirt stretched across his wide chest before tapering down to a narrow waist. Dark chinos skimmed his long, muscular legs, accentuating his height. His look was more corporate mogul than movie star, with a distinct preppy flavor. Watching him stride forward, master of his legal domain, Sarah quickly forgot about her nagging pantyhose.

Stopping in front of her, he extended his hand, and Sarah jumped to her feet, quickly recovering her sense of professionalism.

"Pleased to meet you," she replied, taking his large hand. She studied his face, watching the small lines at the corners of his piercing blue eyes increase with his widening smile. Returning his smile, she continued to lightly pump his hand, utterly distracted by the warmth and strength of it.

"You ready to eat?" he asked, interrupting her thoughts.

"Yes," she managed, quickly withdrawing her hand.

"I understand I have a pretty fearsome reputation at MAG." He quietly laughed, guiding her toward the elevator and pushing the call button. The doors slid open, and he motioned her in. "I'm glad you weren't scared away."

"I don't believe rumors," Sarah said, stepping inside, finding his confidence infectious. "I like to examine the evidence myself before passing judgment."

"Very prudent."

He stepped inside, and the doors slid closed. Sarah examined him out of the corner of her eye while he watched their descent through the back of the glass elevator. She had the strange sensation she'd seen him somewhere before but couldn't think where. Something in his blue eyes and the confident way he carried himself seemed familiar.

"So, what do you think of the studio?" he asked, suddenly turning to her and interrupting her musing.

"It's great," she answered quickly, doing her best to keep her wandering mind focused.

"I'll show you some more of it before we have lunch." The elevator doors slid open, and they made their way through the lobby toward the exit leading out to the lot. He hurried forward to get the door, taking her a little by surprise. She rarely saw such manners in casual LA.

"Thank you." She smiled, trying not to brush against him as she stepped out into the warm afternoon sun.

"My pleasure," he replied, falling into step beside her and leading her into the heart of the studio lot.

"Do you recognize this street?" He gestured toward the faux neighborhood on their left. It looked like a small-town center with false storefronts and an old-time café.

"It's the set from *Hidden Pleasures*."

"You watch it?"

"Only because my roommate makes me."

"Sounds like a weak excuse to me. I think you really like it," he teased.

"I don't know how anyone could like it. The plots are totally unrealistic, and the acting is terrible."

"It's our biggest TV hit," he said with a straight face.

Sarah's smile faltered a bit. "Oh."

"Doesn't say much for the public's taste, now does it?" He winked, making her feel less foolish for criticizing one of their productions.

"No, it doesn't." She laughed.

They headed deeper into the lot, passing numerous sound-stages, trailers, and props. The large door to one soundstage stood open, allowing Sarah to peek inside. Men in shorts and T-shirts, their baseball caps turned backward, tool belts around their waists, worked to construct what looked like the inside of a Renaissance palace.

"It seems like a waste to build all this, only to tear it down in a few weeks," Sarah remarked, taking in the gilded staircase and elaborate chandeliers.

"It's not that great." He pointed to the back of one set, revealing the thinness of the fake stone walls. "Just part of the fantasy."

"Do you like fantasy?" Sarah asked, glancing sideways at him.

He cocked a surprised eyebrow at her, then flashed a suggestive smile. "Do you?"

"It can have its uses," she replied, tossing him a knowing smile. "Any lawyer who's been in a courtroom knows that."

"Touché."

They continued walking deeper into the grid of sound-stages, Jake describing the different shows and movies currently in production. His easy manner surprised her, especially after everything she'd heard from Rachel and Bonnie.

"I find it hard to believe your fearsome reputation," Sarah remarked good-naturedly, enjoying the comfortable familiarity between them.

Jake chuckled, not surprised by the remark. "You're happy with the evidence?"

"I think I need to see more, but my preliminary findings make the original verdict suspect."

"I wouldn't judge too soon."

"You plan to yell at me?" Sarah challenged.

"I don't 'yell.' I'm very direct. MAG assistants don't like direct people," Jake stated simply, without apology.

"No, they don't," Sarah agreed, remembering her own hesitation when it came to answering Jake's call.

They passed a busy soundstage where crew members ran around shouting orders to actors while the cameras stood waiting to roll. Stopping to watch them film a scene, Sarah allowed herself to get caught up in the glamour for a moment, marveling at the famous actors and enjoying the sight of extras in Civil War costumes sitting in folding chairs, reading trade papers.

Finally, they reached the center of the studio and a square, cafeteria-style building where numerous people filed in and out accompanied by the smell of French fries and burgers. She expected Jake to turn toward the building, but he continued past it.

"I thought we were having lunch at the commissary," she said.

"No, we're having lunch at Olivia Hayworth."

"Olivia Hayworth?"

"The formal restaurant on the lot. It's the place to go if you want to see stars."

He turned a corner, leading her down a faux 1940s street toward a regal-looking theater with a fancy marquee. Pulling open the door, he ushered her inside into an eclectic blend of new and old Hollywood style. Booths lined the large picture windows facing the 1940s set, giving the illusion of traveling back in time. The walls in between the windows supported large black-and-white glamour pictures of classic stars, only a few of whom Sarah recognized. The quiet rattle of ice in glasses and the scraping of utensils across plates punctuated the elegant, sedate atmosphere. With a rush of excitement, she eagerly scanned the room, looking for a famous face. Much to her disappointment, only men in dark suits occupied the tables in the mostly empty restaurant.

"Good afternoon, Mr. Rappaport," the attractive young woman at the door practically purred at Jake.

"Hello, Emily. You look lovely today."

His compliment brought a blush to the young woman's face. "Thank you. I have your usual table ready."

"You're the best." Jake flashed the hostess a wide, well-practiced, charming smile, then turned to Sarah. She felt a small flutter in the pit of her stomach and resisted the urge to giggle like a teenage girl. "Shall we?" He motioned for her to follow the hostess.

Warning bells went off in Sarah's mind during the walk

to the booth, near the window. Obviously, he intended to charm her the way he'd charmed the hostess. Did he hope to get information about the arbitration out of her? If so, she'd soon make him realize his mistake.

Sarah slid into the booth, accepting a menu from the distracted hostess who continued to smile at Jake before heading off back across the restaurant.

"So, what brought you here?" he asked, laying his white napkin over his lap.

She leaned her elbows on the table, fixing him with a saucy smile. "You invited me, remember?"

He laughed in a thick, heady tone Sarah found intoxicating. Quickly grabbing her water, she took a sip, hoping to cool the growing heat of her blush. Where had that response come from? It wasn't like her to be smart-mouthed, especially not with opposing counsel.

"What I meant was, what brought you to an entertainment union?"

"It seemed . . . glamorous."

"Is it?"

She thought of the pile of files in her office and her seven-mile commute that took nearly forty minutes every morning and evening. "Today it is."

"I'm glad I could oblige." He leaned his elbows on the table, interlacing his fingers before his face in a serious manner. "So, what do you think about Lion Studios disputing your claim?"

"I think Lion Studios is going to regret it."

Throughout lunch, Jake studied Sarah Steele with a mixture of curiosity and amusement. Despite their opposing views, he enjoyed watching her initial awkwardness give way to an attractive confidence he remembered well from law school. After the way she'd studied him in the elevator, he thought she'd remember him by now. Obviously she hadn't.

"Surely Lion Studios understands the financial impact such a poor interpretation of the Basic Agreement causes actors?" she asked, pushing a strand of her auburn hair behind her ears. She wore it longer than he remembered. It framed her face in delicate waves, highlighting her striking cheekbones and fine nose. Thin-rimmed tortoiseshell glasses ringed her intelligent hazel eyes, emphasizing the natural beauty one didn't usually see in LA.

"Lion Studios is not in the business of securing the financial future of actors. We're in the business of making movies and turning a profit for our investors. Actors are paid for their services. It's up to them to make their pay meet their needs."

"Difficult to do when Lion Studios doesn't pay actors everything they're owed."

"We pay them according to the Basic Agreement."

"I'm afraid Lion Studios and MAG have a slightly different interpretation of the Basic Agreement."

"I'm afraid so." They'd been together for almost an hour, and she still didn't recognize him. *Am I so forgettable?* he thought, swirling the ice cubes in his empty water glass. "We also have a different view of residuals."

"You don't believe actors should be compensated for contributing to the success of a Lion Studios' film?"

Jake shrugged. "Sure, when a film is successful. But actors want to be paid even when a film loses money. They want all of the rewards but take none of the risks. And for what? They don't write the words they say, and they're paid for their day of work. How much more do they honestly expect?"

"Lion Studios is making money from the actors' talent."

Jake laughed. "Talent? Have you seen some of these actors? I hardly call what they have talent."

"That's Lion Studios' fault for hiring them, but that doesn't mean they shouldn't be compensated."

"If they want to be continually compensated for their work, then they should be willing to share in both the profit and the loss. Let them prosper if the film does well, and if it doesn't, they don't get a dime."

"With the questionable studio accounting, you can hardly expect them to trust the studios to share the profit when there is profit," Sarah offered with a light laugh.

"You still don't remember me, do you?"

Her laughter instantly died, and her mouth fell slightly open in surprise. "Remember you?"

"Of course. How could you forget?" He smiled, stretching his arms over the back of the booth and drumming his fingers on the dark leather.

Sarah examined him, a questioning crease forming between her eyebrows. His own smile faltered a bit, along with his pride.

"Law school," he said slowly, fighting his rising irritation to remain polite, especially when the reminder failed to jog her memory. "Dr. Connor's Constitutional Law class. You and I had very different opinions on the First Amendment."

Sarah sat back in the booth, recognition finally dawning

on her pretty face. "Yes, I remember. You seemed to think there should be limits on free speech."

"No, I think people can say what they want but shouldn't complain about the consequences."

"You asked me out afterward, didn't you?"

Why don't you just slap me? Jake thought. She couldn't remember their debate without a hint, but she could remember refusing him without any trouble. "You turned me down flat."

The words came out with more force than he'd intended, but he quickly covered the mistake with a suave smile. "Obviously I've recovered from the rejection."

"Obviously." She laughed nervously, taking another sip of water. He watched her eye him over the rim, more recognition flashing through her eyes as she returned the glass to the table. "Your family owns Rappaport & Rappaport, one of the biggest law firms in Alexandria."

"It's coming back to you now."

Sarah nodded. "Along with the reason I turned you down."

"Oh, really? What was that?"

"You were arrogant." The statement didn't come out as an insult but merely a fact.

"Arrogant?" He started, unsure whether to be insulted or to thank her for her insight into this particular character flaw.

"Very," she replied, the flickers of a teasing smile on her lips. It dissolved his anger, though it didn't smooth the sting to his ego. "Though not so much now."

"You're incredibly honest for a lawyer."

"Or perhaps I'm just a good liar." She put her elbows on

the table, laced her fingers beneath her chin, and offered him a self-assured smirk. "I see you didn't join the family firm after law school."

"I know you won't believe this"—he leaned his elbows on the table, offering her the kind of smile he used to elicit discounts out of perfume-counter saleswomen—"but I didn't want to fall back on my family laurels. I wanted to make my own way."

"It helps when you're already rich."

Jake felt himself falter a little. He'd expected a much more charmed reaction, not this amused, no-nonsense approach. He should have known a woman like Sarah Steele couldn't be charmed.

Her look softened a bit, as though she realized the possible insult of her remark and thought better of it. "But you've certainly succeeded on your own."

I didn't succeed with you, he thought, wondering what it would take to break through that hard black suit to the passionate woman he knew lurked just below the surface. He'd seen the look in her eyes when he'd first stepped out of his office. It was the same look he'd seen after their debate so many years ago, the one he felt compelled to conquer. The only conquest he'd failed to make.

He bit back a curse as the BlackBerry on his waist chirped. "Excuse me a moment."

As he glanced at the message, his irritation instantly increased. He couldn't ignore this e-mail, or one of the biggest productions on the lot would shut down. Pleasure might be calling, but duty came first. He looked up to make his excuses to Sarah, then hesitated, his eyes catching hers. Her flirtatious glance, combined with the slight grin pulling at the corners of her full lips, made him want to throw the BlackBerry out the window and spend the rest of the afternoon talking to her.

The BlackBerry chirped again, demanding his attention. "I'm sorry to cut this short, but it looks like I have to avert a crisis between a producer and the stagehand union."

"I understand. Besides, I have to get back to the office. I can find my own way back if you need to leave."

Jake shook his head. He might be a busy man, but he was also a gentleman. "No, I'll walk you back to your car."

He escorted her out of the restaurant, holding the door open for her. She stepped outside, blinking against the sunlight reflecting off the white Art Deco facades.

"So, you think I'm a privileged rich boy?" he asked with a chuckle, though the question was half-serious. He couldn't get her previous comment out of his mind.

"I shouldn't have said that—it was rude," she apologized, avoiding his eyes.

"Can't blame a person for telling the truth," he admitted, attempting to laugh away her awkwardness.

"The truth isn't always the best defense." She glanced at him, nearly stunning Jake with the way her eyes sparkled in the bright sun.

He imagined her next to him during a drive up Pacific Coast Highway with the top down, her hair flying in the wind. They'd stop for lunch in Malibu and debate law over fish and chips. What a change of pace it would be to spend an afternoon with a woman who wasn't interested in his Hollywood connections or in landing a rich husband. The thought made him want to draw out their time together and get to know her better.

Checking the strange feeling of excitement in his chest, Jake watched her dig the car keys out of her purse, quickly remembering her status as opposing counsel. He might not want their time together to end, but he couldn't make their professional relationship personal. He'd spent too many years building his career to risk it now. Still, he'd caught the subtle flirting, the easy way they'd chatted during lunch, and it gave him hope. Any attraction to her was dangerous, but maybe it had its advantages. After all, there was life after arbitration.

"Let's continue our debate about labor," he offered. "I have two passes to the *Lusitania* premiere tomorrow night. Come with me, and I'll show you some true Hollywood glamour."

She hesitated, obviously surprised.

"We can discuss business," he quickly added.

"Thanks, but I can't."

"Of course you can. People go to premieres all the time." This woman was once again proving a tough nut to crack, but Jake enjoyed a challenge.

"People, not opposing counsel," Sarah reminded him.

The response took Jake by surprise. For a moment he faltered, but he wasn't about to give up so easily. He hated to think he was losing his touch.

"You make it sound like a date." He laughed.

She met his laugh with a nervous smile, edging closer to her car.

"It's just an industry event." He shrugged. "Besides, think about how much it'll impress everyone back home."

She glanced toward the sky, visibly pondering this last suggestion. He almost had her. All he had to do was seal the deal.

"True, but—"

"But nothing. I insist. I'll send a car around to pick you up at your place tomorrow at seven. E-mail me your address. See you tomorrow night."

He turned on his heel, strolling off toward his office, denying her the chance to back out. Pulling open the building's heavy door, he turned for one last look, offering a brief wave before stepping inside.

Sarah slipped into the driver's seat, slamming the door shut behind her.

What just happened?

She leaned against the warm steering wheel, resisting the urge to bang her head against the preformed rubber.

One minute she was a practiced lawyer, the next she was calling him arrogant and being what could only be described as sassy. Who had she just become? Dinah? Sure, Jake Rappaport had been arrogant in law school, but he wasn't today. What had possessed her to say it? Why hadn't she just called him a snake, a flirt? After all, he'd been those things too. In fact, unless she'd imagined it, he'd flirted with her today. Why shouldn't he? It was a more effective strategy for settling claims than calling the other side arrogant and teasing him about her ability to lie. What ability? It didn't exist. What had come over her?

Jake's smile filled her mind, and with it came a sense of panic. *The last time she'd felt like this* . . . No, she didn't feel anything except the need to get back to work and to stop making an idiot out of herself. She started the car but didn't put it into gear. Why had she accepted his offer to go to the premiere? Revenge? Wouldn't a premiere be a great event to write home about, something to torture David with? Was she so petty, or was there another, even smaller-minded reason lingering in the back of her brain?

No. She slammed the car into gear, quickly backing out of the parking space. There was no other reason than revenge. As for Jake's flirting, it was all an act. He was not used to rejection in any form. He was a rich boy, good-looking, and far too sure of himself. He'd turned her off in law school, yet now she found him strangely attractive, especially the way he'd leaned against the back of the booth, confident and successful in a way David had never been. If she'd gone out with Jake in law school, things with David might never have happened.

Who was she kidding? Dating Jake instead of David would have been trading one mistake for another. If things felt awkward now because she'd rejected Jake eight years ago, how awkward would she feel if she'd actually gone out with him?

Stomping on the gas pedal, she launched the car down the ramp onto the freeway. Luckily traffic was moving, a rare event in LA, because she needed the speed and freedom of an open road and music. Sliding back the sunroof to let in the gorgeous California day, she turned on the radio, cranking up the volume on a cruising tune in an effort to drive thoughts of Jake Rappaport from her mind. It didn't work. Despite the sun, the music, and the speed, she couldn't help but feel there was something wrong in accepting his invitation to the premiere.

"I thought you weren't going to the *Lusitania* premiere," Steve said, lounging on the large leather sofa in Jake's office. "You said premieres bored you."

"They do, but I changed my mind." Jake shrugged, signing the last of the memos his secretary had left on his desk.

"Good. I was starting to worry about you. Who are you taking?"

"New attorney at MAG. Sarah Steele."

"A MAG attorney?" Steve Manning stared at his friend in disbelief. "At least tell me she's hot."

"Not in the way *you* like." Jake flipped through the pile of mail on his desk, pulling out a photo Christmas card from the middle of the stack. Framed by cartoon snowmen, his nephew, Dylan, posed in the snow, flashing a wide, slightly toothless smile, while Jake's sister, Terri, and her husband stood just behind him. He hadn't seen his nephew since last Christmas, and the boy had grown, making Jake suddenly feel old.

Jake didn't do photo Christmas cards. What would he take a picture of, his Porsche? Last year he'd have thought it the ultimate achievement worth bragging about. This year it seemed shallow, like so much of LA.

"Then what's the point?" Steve asked, picking up a golf ball from the dish of golf balls on the side table next to the sofa and rolling it absentmindedly between his hands.

"The point is to actually have a conversation with a woman."

Steve stared at him, the golf ball still. "Since when?"

"Since I got tired of discussing the tabloids with the last chick I dated."

"You two broke up almost a year ago." Steve tossed the ball into the air, then caught it. "Time to get over her. There's a whole new crop of starlets waiting for you."

"They aren't new. Just bad clones of the previous crop."

Jake pulled open a large envelope, removing the ruling from his last arbitration against the Extras Union. He'd won a major victory in regard to the payment of overtime. Glancing over the arbitrator's decision, he didn't feel his usual sense of accomplishment, only restless boredom. Shoving the feeling aside, he flipped through the ruling, making notes in the margins. Now wasn't the time to let a little midcareer frustration get in the way of his professional goals.

"So you want to have a conversation—overrated, in my opinion—but it's what you want. Why a lawyer from MAG? You aren't getting soft on labor, are you?"

"Nope. I have a plan." Jake tossed the arbitration award onto his desk, then leaned back in his chair, lacing his fingers behind his head and studying his friend. They'd known each other since their days as assistant counsel in the Lion Studios legal department. They'd even shared a rent-controlled apartment in a questionable part of Santa Monica for a few years. But where Jake took his family fortune in stride while carving out a professional place for himself, Steve was content with his trust fund and the respectable but not astronomical success he'd achieved as Deputy Senior Labor Relations Counsel for Lion Studios. He was quite happy to rest on his laurels and enjoy the Hollywood scene, as long as the scene continued to provide him with a fresh crop of bathing-suit models easily impressed by his job title.

"If I win this arbitration, my promotion to Senior VP is in the bag," Jake said. "What better way to win it than to charm a little info out of the opposing side?"

A wicked smile of approval spread across Steve's chiseled features. "Good idea."

Something inside Jake didn't agree, but he forced it down.

"I know. It's why I'm head of Labor Relations, and you're not." Jake rose, crossing the room to where his putter stood against a wall.

"No, you're head because I have no ambition," Steve corrected with a laugh.

"Too true."

"What makes you think she'll fall for your smooth-guy act?"

"Smooth-guy act?" Jake asked, rolling a white golf ball from the pile next to the wall before taking a couple of practice swings. "What makes you think it's an act?"

"You know what I mean. Working your magic on starlets is like shooting fish in a barrel. A hippie labor lawyer won't be so easy."

"I hope not. I like a challenge. Besides, I know a little something about this one. I knew her in law school." Jake finished his putt, the ball completely missing the cup, much to his surprise.

"You knew her?" Steve put the emphasis on *knew,* clearly conveying his idea of reviving an old relationship.

"She was just a classmate." *But I would have liked to know her better*, Jake thought, though he didn't say it. He sank the next putt, then lined up another. "I asked her out once, but she turned me down."

"Turned you down?" Steve clasped his chest in mock surprise. "I didn't think it was possible."

Jake opened his arms, offering a wide, self-assured smile. "I was not always the god you see before you."

"Obviously. So, what's changed with this particular female?"

"Small-town girl in the big city. It's also like shooting fish in a barrel."

"Sweet." Steve tossed the golf ball back into the dish, then stood. "I have a meeting in fifteen minutes. I'll see you later." He walked out of the office, closing the door behind him.

Leaning the putter back against the wall, Jake returned to his desk, flipping open the arbitration award. He attempted to draft a memo explaining the award to his superiors, but his mind kept returning to Sarah. The playful way she'd looked at him at lunch haunted him. Gone was the hard, revolted look he'd seen in her eyes when he'd asked her out in law school. This time she'd greeted him with an interest he'd felt even in her initial handshake. During lunch, the way she'd teased him, always on the verge of flirting but careful not to cross any lines, gave him hope. Life usually didn't offer second chances, yet here she was, single, beautiful, and as smart as he remembered.

Jake strode to the window and watched as two men maneuvered a large set piece through a soundstage door. Now wasn't the time to get overly sentimental over a woman who barely even remembered him. With a job to do and an arbitration to win, he doubted the head of Lion Studios would approve of his dating the other side until after he won. No, he'd have to make friends with Sarah first, gain her trust along with a few key pieces of information concerning MAG's strategy, before he sealed the deal. After the arbitration, to keep things from getting too complicated, perhaps he could entice her away from MAG. Rumor had it that one of the attorneys in the foreign-distribution department was leaving Lion Studios at the end of the year. It was a prime gig with great pay and no conflict of interest. The trick was to keep Sarah interested in him long enough to avoid being turned down once the arbitration was over.

Jake returned to his desk, punching the intercom button on his phone.

"Yes?" his assistant answered.

"Send Mary in. I have an errand for her."

"Yes, Mr. Rappaport."

He leaned back in his chair, turning it toward the window to take in the Hollywood sign on the hill above the studio. If there was one thing he knew how to do, it was capture a woman's interest.

Chapter Three

Sarah slammed the condo's front door closed, then stormed down the hall to her bedroom. Reaching up under her skirt, she yanked off her pantyhose, hearing them rip in numerous places, but she didn't care. Throwing the mangled nylons into the trash, she pulled off her jacket and tossed it on top of one of the many cartons still piled near her closet. Everything with work had happened so fast, she'd barely had time to unpack more than the basics. One dented box sagged next to the bed, her alarm clock and lamp positioned precariously on top of it.

"Bad day at the office?"

Sarah whirled around to see Dinah leaning against the doorjamb.

"You have no idea." She pulled on her black yoga pants and a T-shirt, then motioned for Dinah to follow her toward the kitchen. After a day like today, chocolate fudge ice cream was a must, even if it meant an extra fifteen minutes of jogging tomorrow morning.

"Oh, try me. I've seen it all." Dinah flopped onto the couch just outside the kitchen.

"You'd think a stunt performer would be happy when I get him sixty thousand dollars in back residuals," Sarah complained, pulling a frozen dinner from the freezer and popping it into the microwave. Watching it spin around, she resisted the urge to sigh. The ice cream would have to wait until she got some protein into her. "No. Instead, he yells at me on his cell phone while he's teeing up on the fifth hole because I didn't get the money fast enough. I've worked for a lot of people, but actors have to be the most insane."

Dinah thought for a moment, her blue eyes studying the ceiling. "I agree, though all Hollywood clients tend to be nuts to some degree."

"I don't know, maybe this town isn't for me." She was thirty-two, single, and eating frozen turkey with a dollop of mashed potatoes. The move to LA might have marginally improved her professional life, but her personal life left a lot to be desired.

"Everyone says that in the beginning. You'll adjust," Dinah encouraged. "How was lunch? Was Jake Rappaport as arrogant as I told you he'd be?"

"No, not really. He's quite nice." Sarah turned her back on Dinah, concentrating on peeling the hot cellophane off the dinner tray. She felt a slight blush creeping up her cheeks, one she hoped Dinah wouldn't notice. "Though you're right about his being a ladies' man. The waitress worked extra hard to get his attention."

"Did *you* get his attention?"

"I must have. He remembered me from law school."

Sarah carried the frozen dinner to the chair next to the couch, kicking off her slippers as she sat down to eat. "I didn't even remember him."

"But he remembered you." Dinah's eyes lit up, and she tucked her legs under her. Sarah remembered this plotting pose from high school and the many detentions they'd endured because of it. "What else did he do?"

"Not much." Sarah shrugged, trying not to show much interest in the lunch, afraid to reveal just how much she'd thought about Jake all afternoon. "He invited me to the *Lusitania* premiere."

"Oh, my goodness." Dinah nearly fell off the couch in excitement. Sarah felt a flutter of panic. The premiere was turning into a bigger deal than she realized. "He has a thing for you."

Sarah shook her head. "He does not have a thing for me."

"Of course he does. He remembers you from law school long after you've forgotten him, he invites you to lunch, then to a premiere."

Sarah tossed the empty dinner tray onto the coffee table, then leaned back in the chair. "He invited me to lunch to discuss a claim. He remembered me because he needs some angle for this case, and he invited me to the premiere because—" Sarah stopped, wondering why he had invited her to the premiere.

"He has a thing for you."

"Definitely not." She grabbed the plastic tray, stood, and stuffed it into the trash can. "Even if I was interested in him, which I'm not, do you know what kind of conflict of interest it would be for a MAG lawyer to date the head of Labor Relations, especially when said lawyer is working on a large arbitration against the studio? I could be disbarred, sanctioned, my career ruined."

Dinah leaned back on the couch, putting her perfectly manicured feet on the coffee table. "Could you switch studios with someone else?"

"Dinah!" Sarah laughed, throwing a small pillow at her friend. "It's still bad. Besides, don't you think it's odd that a man like Jake, who can't be hard up for a date, would ask me to a premiere?"

"No."

"Well, I do. There's something more to this than wanting to catch up with an old classmate. He's trying to manipulate me."

"With a premiere?" Dinah looked skeptical.

"Of course. He makes friends with me, then hopes he can charm some information about the arbitration out of me."

Dinah thought for a moment, drumming her manicured fingers on the arm of the couch. "I don't think so."

"Why not?"

"Because if he remembers you from law school, then he knows you're too smart to be suckered into giving away details."

"Or maybe he thinks he's that good a charmer?"

"Or maybe he's still interested in you."

"No, he can't be." Sarah thought for a moment, pulling the drawstring of her velour yoga pants through her fingers. He couldn't be interested in her, could he? No, it was impossible. However, he had asked her out once before. Sure, it was eight years ago, but he'd asked. Certainly a man like Jake Rappaport didn't moon over some girl who'd turned him down. Still, Sarah couldn't help but feel there was more to Jake's invitation than a friendly desire to show her the glamour of Hollywood—something devious she'd need to be on guard against.

"You could use his interest to your advantage," Dinah suggested.

"I could, if I was that kind of person, but I'm not. However, I think he is."

The doorbell rang, and both women looked at the door.

"Are you expecting someone?" Dinah asked, and Sarah shook her head.

Dinah hopped off the couch, crossing the room to pull open the front door. Around her, Sarah saw a young man in jeans and a T-shirt with the words *Studio Courier* embroidered on it. Dinah signed for a small envelope, then shut the door.

"It's for you, from Lion Studios." Dinah handed her the envelope with a curious look. "How did Lion Studios get your home address?"

"I e-mailed it to Jake this afternoon."

"You gave it to the enemy?"

Sarah shrugged, trying to sound as nonchalant as she could. "He needed to know where to send the car."

"For the premiere?"

"Of course."

Dinah leaned forward, a very serious look on her face. "Most people drive their own cars to premieres, unless they're big stars . . . or they've caught the interest of the head of Labor Relations," she said with a knowing smile.

Sarah ignored the look by ripping open the envelope to reveal a gift card to a trendy Brentwood fashion boutique. The card, along with the amount listed on the back, made her heart race in both excitement and fear.

"Well, what does it say?" Dinah demanded.

" 'I don't know if you have anything to wear,' " Sarah read aloud. " 'Buy a dress on me. See you tomorrow night. Jake.' "

Dinah snatched the gift card out of her hand, turned it over, and let out a low whistle. "You must have made quite an impression on him in law school."

"The kind I didn't want to make. I'll send the card back. I should probably cancel too. The more you talk about it, the worse an idea it seems."

Dinah grabbed Sarah by the shoulders, the excitement in her eyes far outpacing any flutter Sarah might have felt. "You can't cancel. It's the biggest premiere of the season."

"Do you know how wrong it is for me to cavort with opposing counsel?"

"So, don't get personal with him. Just go and enjoy yourself. Besides, everyone in Hollywood schmoozes with everyone else. Why shouldn't you?"

"What if my boss finds out?"

"She's probably been to a hundred of these things. If not, tell her I scored the tickets and went with you."

"And Jake?"

"If you know he's trying to scam you, then you can't be scammed. Go have some fun, enjoy a little Hollywood perk. Think of it as part of your new life. Besides, people drink at premieres. After a couple of drinks, *he* might tell *you* something worth knowing."

"I can't."

"You won't. But if he offers, and you happen to be there to hear it . . ." Dinah's voice trailed off as she dangled the gift card in front of Sarah.

Sarah eyed it nervously, unable to believe the current

situation. In a way Dinah was right. Why not take advantage of the offer to sample some Hollywood glamour? And what if Jake did let something slip? If he wanted to play this kind of game, then why shouldn't she play along?

"I will go," Sarah said with a confident toss of her head.

"You go, girl," Dinah cheered.

"Oh, I will."

"Do you want this?" Dinah held up the gift card. "If you don't, I'll use it."

Sarah playfully snatched the card from Dinah. "This is going back to Jake. I don't want to enjoy myself too much. It might seem a little unethical."

"Good idea."

Sarah yawned, surprised at how tired she suddenly felt. "If I'm going to have a late night tomorrow, I'd better get some sleep tonight."

"You don't want to watch *Hidden Pleasures*?"

"I think I've had enough drama for one day. Good night."

Sarah made her way to her room and closed the door. Thoughts of Jake suddenly filled her mind. She couldn't shake the image of him smiling at her from across the table, or the daydream of running her finger along the strong line of his jaw, tracing it up toward the wavy hair.

It's only a rebound, she thought, heading toward the bathroom.

A man is nice to me, and I instantly think he has a thing for me, she chided herself while brushing her teeth. It was a weakness she needed to conquer. Still, it did seem odd for a man with such a fearsome reputation to suddenly be so nice. Or did he do this with all the women he found attractive?

Sarah rinsed out her mouth, pulled on her nightshirt, then

slipped into bed. She tried reading, but Jake continued to dominate her thoughts. Finally, she flipped off the lamp and rolled over onto her side. The orange glow of the streetlight outside the condo filled her room as she tossed and turned, looking for a comfortable position.

After all her heartache with David she wanted nothing more than to forget about men, to concentrate on her career and build a new life. Sarah sighed. No amount of career success could dampen her desire to find a man who loved and supported her in a way David never had.

Sarah thought of Jake, remembering the way he'd watched her during their discussion. He might have disagreed with her opinions, but he'd never belittled her. She'd seen respect in his eyes when he listened, something she hadn't seen in David's eyes since their last year of law school. Jake's warm, friendly smile filled her mind, along with a strong physical sense of him. She could easily imagine curling up to him, allowing his arms to hold her after a long day at work.

Sarah sat up, smacking the pillow with her fist. No, she couldn't think about him. He was off-limits—way, way, way off-limits. Besides, with all the beautiful starlets in LA, there was no way he could be interested in her. Her wounded mind, still reeling from David's betrayal, was playing tricks on her. Lying on her back, she closed her eyes, feeling the exhaustion of the day overcoming her. As she drifted off to sleep, she thought of Jake, imagining what he would look like in a tuxedo at the premiere.

Jake stood on his terrace with a glass of wine, watching the lights of the Santa Monica pier glisten in the warm evening air. Off in the distance a ship cruised slowly by, parallel to the shore. His sister, Terri, chatted away on the other end of the phone, cataloging her latest volunteer efforts at her son's school.

"I'm sure you find this incredibly boring," Terri apologized.

Jake chuckled. "Not at all. I like hearing about family."

Terri laughed. "Wait, is this the confirmed bachelor longing to hear about the kindergarten Christmas play?"

"Perhaps it is."

She went silent, and Jake caught the sound of a cartoon train in the background.

"You know, the Jackson case is going to be tried in Los Angeles. Dad's been talking about opening a West Coast office. You'd be the perfect person to run it," she offered hesitantly.

Normally Jake wouldn't allow any discussion of his joining the family firm, but tonight he remained quiet. Suddenly the idea didn't sound so unappealing.

"Whose case is it?" Jake asked, giving Terri an opening she couldn't resist.

"Lisa Williams', but she's married with kids and doesn't want to spend four months in LA trying a case. You could talk to Dad about it. Or Derrick. He's coming to LA soon, isn't he?"

"Next weekend." Jake's older brother, Derrick, and his wife and daughter were coming to California for a legal conference, and Jake was scheduled to spend time with them. "What about someone else in the office?"

"I think only Lisa is barred in California."

Another pause. This was dangerous territory. He'd been so hostile about joining the firm, almost everyone in the family had stopped suggesting it. His merely allowing Terri to broach the topic was risky. The minute they hung up, she'd be on the phone to his parents, and it would only be a matter of time before the others started plotting against him. It was one of the disadvantages of being the youngest son: The family liked to gang up on him. Far from being angry, he realized he missed it.

"Jake, you can't remain a bachelor forever," Terri offered, obviously emboldened by Jake's new openness.

"Says who?" Jake joked.

"As a married woman, I say so. Don't you know it's every married woman's job to marry off single people?" She laughed. "Seriously, aren't you tired of Los Angeles?"

The question made him pause. Was he? No, of course not. He'd spent the last eight years building his reputation in the entertainment industry. He wasn't ready to give it up. Or was he?

"I hadn't really thought about it," Jake replied, forcing the momentary doubt from his mind.

"Liar," Terri shot back with a laugh before her voice turned serious again. "Why not join the firm, do some work that really matters, find a nice woman, and settle down?"

"Terri, I have to go."

"Okay, I won't bring it up again, but at least think about it."

"Give my love to Dylan," he said before they said good-bye. Hanging up, he felt slightly guilty for cutting her off.

Jake sat down on a metal patio chair, watching the traffic fly by on the street below. The warm breeze rustled through the palm trees along the now-deserted walking path winding along the edge of the cliff overlooking the beach. He knew Terri was on the phone right now telling Derrick she'd found a chink in Jake's bachelor armor. He imagined the kinds of discussion this would lead to next weekend, and for the first time he didn't care.

Jake finished off his drink, then wandered inside. Flipping on the lights, he took in the black leather and steel furniture he'd once considered a badge of success.

Tonight it seemed cold and hard. The image of Sarah sitting across from him at lunch filled his mind. He'd enjoyed her gentle laugh, the way her eyes lit up during their debate. What would it be like to be able to chat with her without the restrictions of their jobs? For a moment he pictured the two of them sitting on the couch, discussing their day or tossing ideas back and forth about a particular case over a tray of take-out sushi.

"I can't believe I'm thinking about her," Jake said aloud to the empty room. Storming into the kitchen, he rinsed out the glass, then slammed it into the dish rack. It clanked against the metal, and Jake quickly checked it for cracks before putting it back down and heading to his bedroom. Now was not the time to lose his mind over opposing counsel in a major arbitration.

Chapter Four

I should have used the gift card," Sarah groaned to herself, taking in her rumpled appearance in Dinah's full-length mirror. She'd found her only cocktail dress at the bottom of one of her unpacked boxes. Besides its outdated style, a half hour of ironing had failed to remove the wrinkles in the fake velvet.

I should cancel, she thought, her confidence starting to fail at the thought of stepping into a roomful of Hollywood people, looking like some backwater girl. If Jake didn't laugh at her, it would be a miracle. She sighed, knowing she couldn't back out even if she wanted to because she didn't have his cell number. There was nothing to do but suck up her pride, no matter how unfashionable she might look doing it.

The sound of the front door opening and closing offered a small ray of hope.

"I need help," Sarah pleaded, rushing into the living room.

Dinah shot her a wide-eyed look of shock, dropped her

gym bag to the floor, then grabbed Sarah's hand. "Yes, you do. Come on."

Dinah dragged Sarah into her room. "Take that off, and give it to a thrift store."

Sarah quickly obeyed, tossing the dress to the floor while Dinah dug through the contents of her own closet.

"I think this one will work." She pulled out a short black dress with a scooped neckline.

It looked more revealing than Sarah normally preferred, but with less than a half hour to get ready, she was willing to show some skin. "I'll take it."

"Luckily we're about the same size."

"Luckily." Sarah slipped the dress over her head, surprised by how well it fit. Turning to the full-length mirror, she found the dress sexy yet tasteful. It made her legs look long, but because she was shorter than Dinah, the hem wasn't too high. The scooped neck flattered her chest without revealing too much.

"Wow, it looks better on you than it ever did on me," Dinah said from behind her, admiring the dress in the closet-door mirror. "If Jake doesn't already have a thing for you, he will after tonight."

"I hope not," Sarah mumbled, though on some level the forbidden idea appealed to her.

"Do you have shoes?"

"They're the one thing I do have." She hurried across the hall to her room, pulling out a pair of strappy black heels from the bottom of a box marked SHOES. What her wardrobe lacked in style, she more than made up for with her choice of footwear.

"Come on, let's do your hair." Dinah pulled her to the vanity table, pushing her into the chair in front of the mirror.

Sarah hadn't had time to blow-dry her hair this morning, so she'd twisted it into a bun, allowing it to dry during the day. As Dinah pulled out the clip, Sarah shuddered, imagining the unmanageable mess she'd have to force into submission in a short amount of time. To her great surprise, the amber mass fell in soft waves about her face.

"Wow, for once my hair decided to cooperate."

"Sounds like fate to me." Dinah chuckled, leaving Sarah to do her makeup.

She was just applying the last of her lipstick when the doorbell rang.

"I'll get it. You finish getting ready." Dinah peeked back in before heading off to answer the door.

Sarah grabbed her purse, then took one last look in the mirror. The sophisticated reflection staring back at her was a far cry from the wrinkled mess she'd seen a half hour before.

"Here goes nothing," she muttered, then hurried down the hall. Pausing at the end of the hallway, she stood in the shadows listening to Jake politely refuse Dinah's offer of wine. The moment gave Sarah a chance to compose herself. She wanted to appear calm, collected, as if this were just another ordinary evening instead of a questionable outing with opposing counsel.

Looking around the corner, she watched Jake chat with Dinah. He wore an elegant black Italian suit in a stylish cut, reminding her of A-list actors on an awards show red carpet. The perfectly tailored jacket stretched across his wide shoulders, emphasizing his height and muscular frame. Despite the formal attire, a relaxed air of easiness surrounded him, and everything about him oozed polished sophistication combined with confidence.

"Hello, Jake," Sarah said, stepping into the living room. He turned to take her in, and the appreciative look in his blue eyes sent her confidence soaring.

"I should send gift cards more often," he said with a chuckle. A sense of danger, mingled with a schoolgirl crush, gripped her before she steeled herself against the conflicting feelings.

He's off-limits, she silently reminded herself, though she wanted nothing more than to wrap her arms around him and kiss the smile from his lips.

She withdrew the gift card from her purse and held it out to him. "Thank you, but you know I can't accept this. Luckily, I already had a dress."

He slipped the card into his coat pocket, his friendly smile never faltering. "Well, you can't blame a man for trying."

"If you'll excuse me, it was a pleasure meeting you, Jake," Dinah said, backing out of the room but not before giving Sarah a thumbs-up behind Jake's back.

"Shall we?" Jake motioned toward the door.

Sarah led Jake through the complex's courtyard, past the lighted pool. Looking up, she noted a few stars twinkling in the sky. The Santa Ana winds had blown steadily all day, clearing the air and making the evening pleasantly warm.

"This is a very cute place," Jake said, taking in the *U*-shaped building surrounding the pool.

"It's Dinah's condo. We've known each other for years. She's pretty excited to have me as a roommate."

"You plan on getting your own place?"

"Someday, but for the moment I like having the company. Also, being here gives me the chance to get used to living in LA."

He held open the iron front gate, and Sarah hurried past him, inhaling the scent of his cologne. The urge to bury her face in his neck and take a deep breath almost overwhelmed her, but she maintained enough self-control to stroll past him and down the short flight of steps toward the street.

Ahead of her, a shiny black town car idled next to the curb. A dark-suited driver waited patiently by the open back door. For a moment, Sarah had to check her excitement. With the exception of the high school prom, when she and nine other people had rented a limo, this was her first real experience with a chauffeur. There was something very Cinderella-like about the whole experience—and something calculated. The woman in her might enjoy being swept off her feet, but the lawyer suspected Jake's motives. All this was meant to impress her—the car, the gift card, his bespoke suit—and it did, but not enough for her to give away union secrets.

She slipped into the dark interior and scooted to the far side of the backseat. Her logical mind almost deserted her when Jake joined her and the driver closed the door. Being this close to Jake in the confines of the dark backseat sent her senses humming. Glancing at him out of the corner of her eye, she tried to read his reaction, but his face was in shadow. Looking down at his hand resting on the seat between them, she wondered what it would be like to slip her hand into his. She imagined the warm feel of it, the strong fingers curling around hers offering a gentle, playful squeeze.

"You really know how to travel in style," she said, desperate for some kind of conversation to distract her wandering mind.

"Expense account. It's one of the perks of working at Lion Studios. Don't you have an expense account at MAG?" he asked, leaning back against the seat.

"Yeah. I'll use it to buy you an ice cream cone when we're done." Sarah laughed.

"I'll hold you to it."

The driver started the car, and soon they were on their way. In the glint of street lamps and passing headlights, she caught Jake looking at her. His good looks, so captivating during their walk to the car, seemed even more handsome and mysterious in the semidarkness. For a moment she cursed fate for making him opposing counsel. If things were different, perhaps she could fall for a man like Jake. Thinking about his way with the waitress and what Dinah had said, she wondered if she should even entertain thoughts of a relationship with someone who probably wasn't interested in her. Still, there was something more in his eyes than simple disinterested calculation. They held an unmistakable softness evident even in the faint light. Could he fall for her? Feeling her cheeks flush, she quickly looked away, but curiosity forced her to turn back. He smiled, and her heart fluttered.

"Do you go to a lot of premieres?" she asked, trying to reign in her traitorous emotions.

"A few a year. I was lucky to get tickets to this one. Usually I'm only invited when they can't get enough bodies to fill the seats."

"Who wouldn't want to go to a premiere?"

"A lot of people, especially if it's a bad movie."

"I don't believe it."

"It's true. When I was first at Lion, I got a call from the publicity department. A big director had done a film everyone thought would flop. They were having a hard time filling the seats. Our instructions were to invite everyone we could think of."

"So I'm just here to fill a seat?"

"Not tonight. This is one of the hottest premieres of the year. Besides"—he leaned toward her, making her heart beat faster—"you could never be just a seat filler."

All Sarah's romantic notions suddenly disappeared, and she silently chided herself for getting swept up in the moment. This was all a game to him. Now it was time to play along. "Quite the ladies' man, aren't you?" she asked, raising a curious eyebrow.

He sat back, slightly startled, but the smile never left his face. "That's what I love about women who aren't from LA. They don't fall for everything hook, line, and sinker."

"Perhaps, but we can still be impressed."

"I'm happy to hear it."

The town car stopped at the foot of the red carpet, and a tuxedoed man stepped forward and pulled open the door. Outside, thousands of fans screamed from the bleachers, and seemingly hundreds of photographers standing behind the velvet ropes raised their cameras in anticipation. Sarah swallowed hard, shrinking back a little against the seat. Though the crowd wasn't interested in her, the sheer number of spectators was intimidating.

"Look at all those people," Sarah remarked. "I don't know how stars do it."

"They have very large egos." Jake chuckled, then bounded from the car. Turning, he offered her his hand.

Sarah hesitated, still taking it all in. Despite the overwhelming crowd, a thrill of excitement coursed through her.

"Come on, enjoy it," Jake whispered with a wink.

Something in her warned against enjoying this too much, but she decided to ignore it. How often did a handsome man chauffeur a girl like her to a premiere? She placed her hand in his, the warmth of his fingers calming her nerves. The photographers quickly lowered their cameras, and the screaming dropped a couple of decibels as Sarah stepped out of the car. She waved at the crowd for fun, offering a wide, enthusiastic smile to the people who waved back.

"Fun to pretend, isn't it?" Jake whispered, waving along with her.

"Yes, it is."

Their limo drove off, and another quickly pulled up, filling the air anew with a sense of anticipation.

"Let's watch the professionals do it." Jake maneuvered Sarah off to a place on the side with a good view of the star emerging from the depths of the sedan.

Rick Daniels, star of *Hidden Pleasures,* stepped out, a leggy blond ten years his junior quickly joining him. The red carpet broke into a frenzy of activity punctuated by the continuous strobe of flashbulbs. The flashes lit up the blond's shimmering gold dress as a deafening chorus of "Rick" rose from the pool of photographers begging the actor to look their way.

"It's like a feeding frenzy," Sarah said with a laugh, watching Rick and his date strike a number of poses for the photographers.

"The stakes are high. The right photo can earn those cameramen a lot of money."

The photographers' fierce competition to nail the perfect shot was matched only by the screaming fans holding up pictures and pens, hoping for Rick to walk by. Sarah watched in awe while Rick paused to sign autographs before his publicist guided him toward the press line.

"I guess I haven't really arrived," Sarah said, giggling and watching Rick stop to do an interview with one of the entertainment TV shows.

"Be grateful," Jake whispered, his warm breath tickling her skin, sending a small shiver down her spine. "All this attention isn't what it's cracked up to be. Shall we?"

He motioned toward the theater, taking her by the elbow and leading her past the line of reporters. Sarah did her best not to gawk, but the sheer thrill of being in the midst of the excitement on the red carpet was almost overwhelming.

The theater sat in the heart of Hollywood in an Art Deco building left over from the golden age of movie palaces. The lobby resembled a European palace with gilt decorations accented by a large crystal chandelier. The magnificence of the decor was matched only by the magnificence of the stars milling about.

"It's kind of exciting." Sarah smiled, noting the dizzying number of celebrities mingling in the crowd.

"Kind of." Jake nodded. "Come on, let me introduce you to a few people, give you something really exciting to tell your friends about."

As they moved through the crowd, she noticed a strange ennui lingering in his eyes and attributed it to his experience in Hollywood. This might be her first premiere, but it was probably his hundredth, the glamour having worn off for him years ago. Despite his strange look, Sarah appreciated the way he made the experience a memorable one for her by introducing her to a number of co-workers and a few stars. Any regrets she still held about moving to LA or attending the premiere quickly disappeared. Nothing in Richmond could compare to this, and suddenly all the traffic and the agony of moving across the country seemed worth it.

They mingled for a while before making their way into the theater to find their seats. Sarah walked slowly down the aisle, taking in the elegance. The ornate lobby was nothing compared to the grandeur of the theater itself. Gilded plaster swags hung over the thick red curtain of the proscenium arch. Murals of angels and clouds reminiscent of a Renaissance cathedral decorated the ceiling around the large chandelier. People filled the balcony situated on the back wall, and most stood, craning their necks to see the numerous stars sitting in the first few rows.

"Impressive, isn't it?" Jake asked.

"Very," she replied, looking up to study the elaborately painted ceiling. "Certainly a cut above the mall multiplex."

They took their seats just as the lights dimmed. The movie was a holiday blockbuster high on action and low on plot, but Sarah hardly noticed. Her mind was too distracted by Jake's presence. Despite the surroundings, the evening, her dress, and her law degree, she suddenly felt like a teenager on a first date with her high school crush. When Jake's elbow accidentally brushed hers, it sent a shock through her entire body. She quickly moved her arm, clasping her hands in her lap and tucking in her elbow to keep from accidentally brushing against him again. She stayed that way through most of the picture, only moving when her arm fell asleep halfway through. Despite not touching Jake, she was always aware of him next to her, noting every time he changed positions or reacted to a humorous line. No matter how many times she pulled her attention back to the film, it kept wandering to Jake.

All too soon the credits began to roll, and the lights came on, causing the theatergoers to break into loud applause.

"Did you like it?" Jake asked, leaning toward her.

"Yes, it was very good," she lied. The last two hours had passed in a haze of costumes and special effects, and the only things she remembered about the movie were a man, a woman, and a sinking ship.

Luckily, they didn't have a chance to discuss the film during the walk to the after party in the hotel next door. Too many people stopped to talk to Jake, asking him about different basic agreements or wanting to discuss some trouble on a set. While he answered questions about labor contracts or promised to look into an urgent matter first thing in the morning, she stood quietly next to him, listening to the strong cadence of his voice. His ability to move so easily among producers and studio executives impressed her. She hoped it wouldn't take long for her to develop the same kind of confidence at MAG.

As she stepped into the hotel's grand ballroom, the sheer expense laid out for this one party quickly astounded her. The ballroom was decorated to resemble an elegant ocean liner from the early days of transatlantic travel. Models hired for the evening stood around dressed in Edwardian finery, lending only a small amount of credibility to the atmosphere.

"Do you want something to drink?" Jake asked.

"Sure. How about some white wine?"

"Whatever the lady wishes. Meet me outside?" He pointed to the open doors leading to a stone terrace with a view of Hollywood.

"Okay," she replied before Jake disappeared into the crowd.

Maneuvering through the growing throng, she stepped outside, taking a deep breath of the cool evening air. Crossing the terrace, she leaned her elbows on the cold stone railing to admire the view. The ballroom sat at the top of the Renaissance Hollywood Hotel at the corner of Hollywood and Highland. From here Los Angeles spread out in all its twinkling nighttime glory. On the street below, cars slowed to take in the famous theater, flashbulbs illuminating the night as tourists stopped to take pictures of what remained of the premiere. The warm glow of street lamps was lost in the dazzling white light from the marquee of a competing theater across the street. Despite all the traffic and smog, at a moment like this, on an evening as magical as this, the charm of the city made itself known.

"Beautiful view, isn't it?" Jake remarked, handing her a glass of wine.

"Very."

"I'm glad you're enjoying yourself. I love watching the sparkling eyes of newbies." He winked, offering a subtle reminder of the risky game she continued to play. In spite of the evening's thrills, she had to stay on guard and not give anything away. Offering him a sly smile, she knew it was time to turn the table and take the upper hand.

"It seems that a studio with enough money to spend on parties like this can spare a few extra dollars to pay residuals."

"No fair talking business tonight." Jake laughed.

"I have to talk business. How else can I justify being here to my boss?"

"Don't tell her you were here. First rule of accepting perks is to not tell anyone you're accepting perks."

"Is that the way it's done at the studios?"

"That's the way it's done everywhere."

She crossed her arms, shooting him a disbelieving look. "So, you're saying I'm here because I'm greedy like everyone else?"

He shrugged, obviously refusing to take her concern seriously. "No, you're enjoying a nice evening with an old friend."

"We're hardly old friends."

"Classmates, then. Whatever you want to call it." He leaned closer to her, the heat from his skin taking the edge off the slight chill of the night. "Relax. I'm not trying to pick your brain for information."

Liar, she thought, returning his smile. Though her better sense told her to step back, she leaned in closer, her bare arm tantalizingly close to the silk of his suit. "Still, it does create an interesting conflict of interest, one a studio might take advantage of."

"You think I'd stoop so low?" His hot breath brushed her cheek, making her realize just how close to each other they stood.

"I've seen your rebuttal argument. It's possible," she teased, taking a small step back.

He was about to respond when a leggy blond with a top

cut too low and a skirt hemmed too high suddenly slid up to him.

"Jake."

"Caitlin," he greeted in a less than enthusiastic voice, downing the last of his drink.

"You didn't tell me you were coming tonight," she pouted, sliding in between Sarah and Jake while leaning forward to give him a perfect view down her blouse. Sarah watched, resisting the urge to roll her eyes at the entertaining spectacle.

"Why would I tell you I was coming?" Jake asked in a stern voice Caitlin easily dismissed.

"Why wouldn't you, you tease? I haven't seen you since the Nick Clark premiere last January. Remember?" she asked suggestively.

A slight, knowing smile tugged at the corners of his lips, indicating he obviously remembered what must have been a very pleasant evening.

Sarah leaned back against the wall, offering Jake an amused look that quickly snapped him out of his blissful recollection.

Jake stepped back from Caitlin, recovering his sense of professionalism. "Sarah Steele, this is Caitlin Marks."

Caitlin looked Sarah over, sizing her up as a potential rival. "So, what do you do?"

"I'm an attorney at the Movie Actors Guild."

The girl's eyes suddenly lit up. "I've been trying to get my MAG card. It's so difficult. Maybe you can help?"

"I'd love to," Sarah lied, "but I'm new at MAG, and I don't deal with membership issues."

The girl's smile faltered a bit. "But aren't you trying to be an actor?"

"No."

"A writer?"

"No."

"A director, then. I know a director who works at one of the unions. The stunt one, I think."

"No, I'm just an attorney." Sarah shrugged.

Caitlin's brow scrunched in an effort to process this obviously inconceivable idea, but she didn't waste too much time on the mental exercise. Quickly dismissing Sarah as useless to her career, Caitlin turned back to Jake, who struggled to suppress a laugh.

"Jake, maybe you can help me by putting in a word with the casting director at Lion Studios."

"I'd love to, but I don't deal with those people. However, if I ever talk to them, I'll definitely mention your name." He smiled to cover the obvious lie, but Sarah saw that, for the first time tonight, his smile did not reach his eyes.

An awkward silence fell between them before Caitlin's cell phone chirped. She snatched the rhinestone-bedecked phone from her equally glittery evening bag, her large lips pursed as she looked at the screen.

"I have to go. My friend is here, and she has someone I have to meet. Jake, don't be a stranger. You have my number." She squeezed his arm playfully before walking off across the terrace, a noticeable wiggle in her hips.

"You have very interesting friends," Sarah said with a wry smile.

He ran a hand through his hair, refusing to meet her eyes. "She's hardly a friend."

"Not even after last January?"

"I barely remember last January."

"That doesn't bode well for me, then, does it?" The question surprised Sarah as much as it seemed to surprise Jake, who pinned her with a suddenly sincere gaze.

"I think Caitlin gave you the wrong impression of me."

Sarah studied him for a moment, biting back a retort about Caitlin giving her the correct impression of him. It was obvious from the look in his eyes that he wanted her to think the best of him, a desire stemming from something more than wanting a good professional relationship with her. He held her gaze, giving her a chance to notice the dark flecks in his blue eyes. They were soft, tender, drawing her in, pulling her forward, closer, toward something imperceptible she could almost taste.

"There you are. I need to talk to you." A handsome man about Jake's age came up behind him, slapping him on the shoulder. Judging by the slick smile on his face and the way he winked at a passing waitress, Sarah got the feeling he was a little too aware of his good looks. "One of the MAG lawyers contacted me right after you left, demanding we pay the balance of Nick Clark's contracted salary."

"Have we paid him?" Jake asked, irritation evident in his voice.

"No, and now Clark is saying he won't do publicity until he receives payment. The producer is flipping out because Clark's interview with *Hollywood TV* is tomorrow. What's an A-list star like Clark doing getting MAG involved? Doesn't he have his own lawyers?"

"Have you tried simply paying the performer what you contractually agreed to pay him?" Sarah asked with a smile. The man turned to her with narrowed eyes. If looks could kill, she'd have dropped dead, but instead of turning away, Sarah continued to smile brightly. She knew his type well and refused to be bullied. Over the man's shoulder, Sarah noticed the amused look on Jake's face.

"Steve, may I introduce Sarah Steele? She's the new attorney at MAG I was telling you about."

"Pleased to meet you," Sarah said, holding out her hand.

Steve took it, a slight redness creeping over his features, but she couldn't tell if it was anger or embarrassment.

"Steve Manning," he mumbled, dropping her hand and turning to Jake. "We need to talk."

"Go ahead, Jake. I should be getting home anyway," Sarah offered, not wanting to make any enemies at Lion Studios.

Jake sidestepped his friend. "Wait, don't go. This will only take a moment."

"No, I have an early meeting tomorrow. I can't be tired."

Jake studied her with a look of disappointment. Obviously torn, he didn't want her to leave, but there was no logical argument for her to stay. He dug the valet ticket out of his pocket and held it out to her. "Take the car. I'll get a ride home with Steve."

She hesitated before taking it, reluctant to bring the evening to an end yet relieved at the same time. "Thank you for a lovely, insightful evening." Sarah strode toward the ballroom, fighting the desire to give Jake one last parting look.

Jake watched Sarah go, resisting the urge to punch Steve.

"I thought I'd save you. Didn't you see Caitlin? She was practically throwing herself at you." Steve leaned against the stone railing, oblivious to the view.

"I'm not particularly interested in what Caitlin has to offer."

"In that case, mind if I show an interest?"

"Go ahead." Jake motioned to where Caitlin stood near the bar. "Now, what about Nick Clark's payment?"

Steve adjusted his tie, smiling across the terrace at Caitlin, who wiggled her acrylic nails at him. "We can discuss it in the morning."

"Thanks, Steve. You're a true friend," Jake sarcastically replied.

"Hey, you may not care about your career, but I do. No use having the boss see you so cozy with the enemy." Steve motioned to where Larry Allen, President of Studio Operations and Jake's boss, stood, watching Jake and Steve.

"What are you talking about?" Jake caught Larry's eye, offering him a nod in greeting before Larry resumed his conversation with an older woman from the production side of studio operations. "I told you why I invited her."

"Are you sure that's why?" Steve asked, cocking a suggestive eyebrow.

"You don't think I'm interested in a MAG attorney, do you?"

"I don't know, but you two looked a little too cozy for a business relationship."

"It's all part of my plan. The more special a woman feels, the more likely she is to reveal something," Jake replied, ignoring the way the statement bothered him.

"Did she reveal anything?"

"No."

"Better luck next time."

"What makes you think there'll be a next time?"

"Because, unlike me, you're tenacious. Just make sure you

know exactly what it is you're going after. Now, if you'll excuse me." Steve clapped him on the back before heading off toward Caitlin.

Jake turned toward the view, knowing he should be inside the ballroom schmoozing with Larry Allen, but he felt reluctant to move. His hesitation surprised him. Last week he'd have been working the crowd, making contacts while impressing the bosses. Tonight everyone seemed as fake as Caitlin's nails. Everyone except Sarah.

The image of Sarah in her black dress seized his mind. When she'd first stepped into the living room to greet him, he'd almost rushed forward to take her into his arms and cover her full, inviting lips with his. He'd forced himself to keep his distance from her in the car, though her warm, lavender scent drove him wild. Even during the film, he couldn't concentrate on the plot, not with her sitting so close. No woman had ever had such a powerful effect on him before.

Jake ran a hand through his hair, forcing his attention back to the party. What was he doing thinking about Sarah? Any relationship with her other than a professional one would ruin everything he'd spent the last eight years building. Though suddenly those accomplishments didn't seem quite so impressive. The feeling hit him as powerfully as the sight of Sarah leaning toward him while they spoke tonight, the delicate line of her neck tantalizingly close to his fingers.

Snatching a cocktail from a passing server, he took a deep sip, the burning sensation in his throat barely diluting his raging emotions. No matter what kind of momentary boredom he might imagine he felt, he wasn't ready to be unemployed or disgraced in front of the studio labor community over some whim from his past. No, when he was ready to leave Lion Studios, he'd do so on his terms. Of course, he'd also see to Sarah Steele on his terms, though he needed to be a little more cautious in the future. For now, he needed a new strategy, a way to win her over and to give him an edge.

Chapter Five

Sarah rested her head against her hand, struggling to stay awake while she scrolled through her e-mails. Though she'd arrived home at a decent time the night before, she hadn't been able to fall asleep for hours. No matter what she did or thought about, she couldn't get Jake out of her mind. The image of him in his elegant suit with his hair swept back off his handsome face, along with the confident way he'd moved through the party, haunted her.

Why, after all these years, was he having this effect on her? She'd easily dismissed him in law school, but now she couldn't stop thinking about him. This was no time to lose her head over a man who was way off-limits. Besides, after her disaster with David, hadn't she learned her lesson about untrustworthy men? Leave it to her to fall for a man who was trying to use her. Was she really that pathetic?

"You look like you had a rough night."

Sarah looked up to see Rachel lounging in her office doorway. "I didn't sleep well."

"Did you get the invitation for Studio Payroll House's annual holiday party?"

"I don't remember. When is it?"

"Tonight."

"Tonight? I guess I can't go," Sarah replied, stifling a yawn.

"Of course you can. Most people RSVP at the last minute." Rachel handed Sarah a flier with the party's information. It was being held at the Hotel Beverly Hills, not far from MAG's mid-Wilshire location.

Sarah glanced down at her dark pants and red sweater, thinking she'd look a lot better if she hadn't hit the snooze button five times that morning. "I'm not really dressed for an industry party."

"Who is? It's a pretty casual affair. If nothing else, enjoy the free dinner and the door prizes. Plus, it's a good chance to meet all the people you only talk to on the phone."

"Is it really all right to RSVP this late?"

"Sure."

Sarah thought for a moment. With Dinah in San Diego for a press junket, there wasn't exactly anyone to run home to. Why not go to the party? It was a good excuse to skip another date with a frozen dinner.

"All right, I'll go."

"Good." Rachel moved to say more, but Sarah's buzzing intercom cut her short.

"Yes?" Sarah answered, mouthing "Thanks" to Rachel before she disappeared around the corner.

"It's Bonnie. Can you grab the *Tidal Wave* file and come to my office?"

"Sure." The line went dead, and Sarah felt her stomach tighten. She hadn't mentioned the premiere to Bonnie or cleared it with her to make sure it was allowed. Had she found out? Grabbing the thick file, Sarah made her way down the hall to her boss' office, nervous adrenaline ending her need for caffeine.

"Come on in," Bonnie instructed, motioning toward the chairs in front of her desk. Sarah took a seat, balancing the large file on her lap. "I heard from the arbitrator today. It's all set for the eighteenth."

"December 18?" Sarah asked, struggling to control her shock.

"Yeah, we were lucky to get such a quick date. The MAG president is eager to see this one settled."

"Do we really want to rush it?"

"We don't have a choice." Bonnie leaned back in her chair. "When one studio realizes they can get away with something, they tell the other studios. Pretty soon half the town is violating the Codified Basic Agreement. Sets a bad custom-and-practice precedent. No, we have to hold this arbitration as soon as possible in order to clarify the statute and nip this in the bud before it spreads."

Sarah fingered the edge of the file. She wasn't one to shrink from professional challenges, but to arbitrate a claim she knew virtually nothing about with only three weeks to prepare was tantamount to career suicide. "Maybe one of the other attorneys should handle the file?"

"Normally I'd assign it to a more senior attorney, but with the number of high-profile arbitrations coming up in the next two months, there's no one left to give it to. Besides, if you could handle Taylor Manufacturing, you can handle Lion Studios."

Sarah felt the knot in the pit of her stomach tighten.

Maybe now was the time to explain how a minor technicality, not her superior skill as an attorney, had helped her win a major verdict against Taylor Manufacturing on behalf of the workers' union.

"As long as you have faith in me," Sarah replied through a forced confident smile. Despite her desire to spill the beans, she knew it was easier to feel like a fraud than to have everyone know she was a fraud.

"I do. You're the first attorney we've had who's been able to settle claims with Lion Studios. What's your secret? You dating Jake or something?" Bonnie laughed, tossing the *The Hollywood Reporter* across the desk. It landed faceup in front of Sarah, open to the second-page coverage of the *Lusitania* premiere. It took all of Sarah's strength not to fall out of her chair in shock. There, in the largest photo, for all the world to see, were Sarah and Jake standing behind Rick Daniels on the red carpet. Luckily they weren't touching, but it was obvious he was whispering something to her.

"My roommate, Dinah, is a publicist at Lion Studios. She scored the tickets. In fact, she's standing just outside the frame. We ran into Jake there. I think he was explaining to me at this point how premieres work. I really didn't see him again after the red carpet," Sarah said in a rush, thankful for Dinah's pre-arranged fib. Her mind would have gone blank without it, and she made a mental note to buy Dinah a box of chocolates in thanks.

Bonnie cocked one curious, well-manicured eyebrow. "You didn't tell me you and Rappaport were on such friendly terms."

"We're not. We had a few classes together back in law

school, but I hadn't seen or talked to him until our lunch the other day." At least that wasn't a lie.

"Well, whatever you're doing, keep it up, because it's working. It's about time someone around here made nice with Jake Rappaport. I don't suppose you know anyone at Summit Studios?"

Sarah shook her head.

"Too bad."

Sarah slowly unclenched her viselike grip on the edge of the *Tidal Wave* file. "It's okay to go to premieres, isn't it?"

"Sure. My friends at Mountain Pictures invite me all the time. You have to take the perks where you can get them. Now, tell me what you've found so far in your research for *Tidal Wave*."

Bonnie and Sarah spent the next half hour going over the file, giving Sarah the opportunity to think of something other than Jake. Discussing the claim, Sarah surprised herself with how much she knew about the file as well as about the MAG Basic Agreement. She'd spent a number of hours with the manager of the residuals department learning how residuals worked and studying the language governing their payment. The hard work had paid off, and by the end of her meeting with Bonnie, she felt more confident about preparing for the arbitration.

"I think that just about does it for today," Bonnie said, drawing their meeting to a close. "Are you going to the party tonight?"

"Yes. Rachel just gave me the flier."

"Great." The phone rang, pulling Bonnie's attention to the latest legal fire to put out. Sarah made her escape, hurrying to her office.

Throwing the *Tidal Wave* file on top of her desk, she fell into her chair. Why had she freaked out when Bonnie joked about her having a friendly relationship with Jake? They didn't have any kind of relationship. They never had. So why did she feel so guilty? Bonnie was right. Being friendly with Jake might help resolve claims, but somehow having her boss' permission made Sarah nervous. A hostile policy toward the other side would have kept things more clear-cut.

Turning to her computer, she moved the mouse, bringing the screen back to life. Scrolling through her e-mails, she spotted a message from Jake asking her to call him with the answers to a couple of questions. Instead of calling, she dashed off an e-mail reply. The last thing she needed was more distractions. What she needed was work. Flipping open the *Tidal Wave* file, she dove in. After an hour of hard work, she felt her usual level of control return, bringing with it some much-needed perspective.

Sarah stepped out of the car, taking in the impressive façade of the renowned Hotel Beverly Hills. Shaking her head, she reluctantly surrendered her keys to the waiting valet, still struggling to get used to this very common LA practice. Hurrying inside the sleek hotel, she quickly caught up with Rachel and a number of other MAG staff in the lobby. They squeezed into a full elevator, spilling out into a large hallway when the doors opened on the top floor.

"I can't believe the number of people here," Sarah remarked to Rachel as they stepped into the check-in line.

"It's the working stiff's highlight of the holiday season. Anyone who's nobody in Hollywood attends."

Good, then Jake won't be here, Sarah thought, surprised by how much the idea disappointed her.

Glancing around at the crowd, she caught a glimpse of the entrance to the Tiki Mai Tai restaurant, one of the most famous old Hawaiian clubs from the 1950s.

"After the party I have to sneak into Tiki Mai Tai and steal a little paper umbrella. I've never been in there," she whispered.

"Then you have to go. The place is hilarious. Very retro," Rachel replied, leading her into the massive ballroom.

All around the room, people stood together in small groups, laughing and talking over the Christmas tunes blaring from the DJ's speakers. In the background, through a large row of windows, the holiday lights of Beverly Hills twinkled in the darkness. Sarah scanned the guests, struggling to see beyond the ten or so people standing directly around her. Hopefully, if Jake were here, he'd have as much trouble spotting her as she had spotting anyone she knew.

"I'm starving. Let's eat," Rachel called over the noise, walking off toward the food station at the far end of the ballroom. Sarah followed, struggling not to lose Rachel in the crush of people. They grabbed plates, then made their way through the buffet. Sarah marveled at the selection— everything from miniature hot dogs to Thai food, all from the restaurant of a famous Beverly Hills chef.

"Is the food always this elaborate?" Sarah asked, snagging a couple of spring rolls.

Rachel shrugged, examining a shrimp skewer. "Yeah. Studio Payroll spares no expense."

Sarah shook her head in disbelief. No holiday party she'd ever been to before could compare to this.

When they'd filled their plates, they found two spaces at a high table near a wall. After they'd introduced themselves to everyone else at the table, Rachel immediately struck up a conversation with a handsome payroll administrator from a small production company. While he plied Rachel for information about the MAG Basic Agreement, Sarah stood politely by, taking in as much information as she could while enjoying a spicy Thai salad wrap.

"I'm going to the bar," Sarah announced, her tongue on fire. "Do you want anything?"

"Nothing, thanks," Rachel answered, then turned back to her hunk of a payroll administrator.

Sarah made her way through the crowd toward the nearest bar. Stepping into line behind a couple of young secretaries, she inspected the nearby dessert table with its fabulous selection of cheesecakes and tartlets. Between the gift baskets pouring into the office and the constant parties, she'd lost all hope of avoiding the five-pound holiday weight gain.

"What'll you have?" the bartender asked when Sarah finally reached the bar.

"Diet Coke."

"What's the point, with all this food?" a familiar voice said with a chuckle.

She turned to see Jake standing behind her. He quickly maneuvered to her side, resting his elbow on the elevated bar and watching Sarah take her soda from the young bartender. Suddenly the temperature in the room rose ten degrees, while the burning sensation from the Thai food disappeared.

Jake looked as good as she remembered from the premiere. He was dressed in dark slacks paired with a blue shirt elegantly tailored to flatter his wide shoulders. He'd probably worn a tie earlier in the day, but it was gone now, his top button open to reveal the smooth skin where his throat met his chest. Over the sweet smell of the maraschino cherries on the bar she caught the heady musk of his cologne.

"I prefer diet to regular," she replied, trying to ignore the sly smile pulling at the corners of his lips.

"Then why not throw in a little rum? Spice it up a bit?"

"I don't like things spicy at work-related events."

"Why not? Everyone else here is spiced. It helps with the networking."

"Are you spiced?"

Jake raised a suggestive eyebrow. "A little."

"Well, I'm not. After all, there's networking, and then there's networking." The teasing tone in her voice surprised her and seemed to embolden Jake, who fixed her with a look of delicious victory.

"What kind of networking did you have in mind?" He stepped a little closer so she could hear him over the DJ's cheesy Christmas carols.

She was about to offer a wicked reply when the man standing behind her cleared his throat. She stepped away from the bar, and, much to her surprise, Jake followed, his blue eyes taking her in with an appreciative glance. Sarah took a sip of her soda in an effort to regain her former calm. Suddenly, Bonnie's suggestion to remain friendly with Jake came to mind. Friendly was one thing, but if Sarah gave in to even one of the romantic thoughts racing through her mind, she wouldn't have a job tomorrow morning. It was time to make this very personal conversation professional.

"This doesn't seem like your type of event," Sarah said casually, careful to keep the flirtatious tone out of her voice. Jake stepped a little closer as an older woman passed behind him on the way to the dessert table.

"What kind of event do I seem right at?"

A small shiver raced up her spine at the deep, rich tone of his voice. His hooded, mischievous eyes bored into her, increasing the heat of the room. What would it be like to toss aside her soda, grab him by the shirt, and taste his smirking lips?

"You seem more the exclusive VIP party type, not the working stiff's free event," she stammered, trying to sound confident.

"I enjoy any party where I can network with colleagues, even those who don't return my phone calls." He took a sip of his drink, offering her a playfully accusing sidelong glance.

"I e-mailed you."

"It's not the same. I enjoy hearing your voice."

Sarah took another sip of her soda, struggling not to choke. Had he just said what she thought he'd said? No, it was impossible. Jake knew the risks of getting involved with opposing counsel. He was teasing her, acting like the playboy she'd pegged him for at the premiere. Yet another reason to keep their relationship strictly professional.

"*Your* voice has gained quite a reputation in our office," she said.

"Really?"

"Yes, you're known as a screamer."

He threw back his head and laughed, a deep, throaty laugh Sarah found enticing.

"I think I've been greatly misunderstood."

"You deny yelling at people?"

"No, I deny yelling at anyone at MAG."

"What about Rachel?"

"All right, I confess, I yelled at her once, but she deserved it."

"And the secretaries?"

"I'm straight and to the point. Some people call that curt. I call it professional. Besides, it always helps to put a little fear into your opponent."

"I'm not afraid of you," Sarah challenged, her heart racing as he stepped a little closer, the heat from his skin making her almost dizzy.

"I'm glad to hear it," he replied in a low voice, and the remainder of Sarah's tart replies died on her tongue. His eyes met hers, studying them in an intimate way. Despite the crowded room, the tacky decorations, and the colleagues walking by, Sarah leaned toward him, her breath catching as he, too, leaned forward, his hair falling over his forehead in a playful way.

"Jake Rappaport, good to see you again," Bonnie said, suddenly appearing at Jake's elbow.

Without missing a beat, Jake turned to Bonnie, offering his hand and his trademark winning smile. "You too, Bonnie Weston. How's your son?"

While they exchanged pleasantries, Sarah marveled at his ability to shift gears so seamlessly. What she wouldn't give for a fifth of his self-confidence right now. After having her boss walk in on their cozy little conversation, she felt anything but confident. They hadn't done anything, yet she felt guilty, as if her mother had walked in on her in the basement during a make-out session in high school.

Suddenly Bonnie turned to her. "Sarah tells me you two went to law school together."

"Yes," Jake said, his smile never faltering. "She was a great student. Too bad you got to her before I could. She'd make an excellent addition to Lion Studios."

"Thankfully she has a passion for labor, don't you, Sarah?" Bonnie asked.

Sarah forced a wide smile onto to her face. "Definitely. I'm not a corporate type."

"That's Lion Studios' loss." Jake raised a glass to the women. "If you'll excuse me, ladies, I see a friend of mine from Screen Dreams. Happy holidays."

He headed off across the room, shaking hands with another gentleman a few tables away.

"Are you sure you two didn't have something going back in law school?" Bonnie remarked with a seasoned lawyer's skill for hunting down information.

"No, I barely knew him. We only had a class or two together." Sarah took a large drink of her soda, hoping it made her appear cool and calm.

"You looked pretty intense. What were you talking about?"

"His habit of yelling at MAG people."

"You are brave." Bonnie leaned back, impressed, the suspicious look in her eye disappearing. "Well, if you can get him to stop yelling, by all means, try. The secretaries will certainly appreciate it. I'll see you later."

Bonnie walked off, and Sarah debated asking the bartender to add a little "spice" to her diet soda. Looking around the room, she wondered who else from MAG had seen her flirting with Jake. No, she hadn't been flirting, simply chatting. Still, if Bonnie had taken it the wrong way, who else would?

Scanning the crowd, her eyes caught Jake's. She quickly looked away, but something, she couldn't say what, drew her back. He smiled, not his playboy smile, but a genuine smile she felt in her stomach.

Desperate to get away, she hurried to the table where Rachel continued to laugh with the payroll administrator. Sarah tried to look interested in the conversation, but her senses remained fixed on Jake. Somehow, she always knew where he stood, catching glimpses of him from the corner of her eye. She fought the urge to mingle and "accidentally" bump into him by staying firmly rooted to the table and laughing at the payroll administrator's alcohol-fueled dumb jokes.

Eventually, the crowd began to thin. Sarah looked at her watch. It was almost ten, and she had an early conference call in the morning.

"I'll see you tomorrow, Rachel," Sarah offered.

"Okay," Rachel mumbled without taking her eyes off her handsome new friend.

Sarah wandered out into the hallway toward the elevator, hesitating at the door to Tiki Mai Tai, debating whether or not to sneak inside and steal a paper umbrella. Noticing a pint glass full of the classic plastic swizzle sticks at the untended bar, she figured now was as good a time as any to snatch a souvenir. Her father had a collection of swizzle sticks from all the old bars. He'd love to get one from Tiki Mai Tai in his Christmas stocking.

Glancing around to make sure no one was looking, she hurried to the polished wooden bar and helped herself.

"I think you're supposed to order a drink," a laughing male voice said. She whirled around to see Jake standing behind her, mock accusation in his eyes.

"Shh!" she hissed, checking to make sure his loud proclamation hadn't attracted any unwanted attention from the wait staff. "Are you trying to get me into trouble?"

"No, but this *is* delicious dirt. What do you think this kind of information might buy me?"

"Do you mean blackmail?" Sarah laughed, relaxing. Perhaps all her recent worrying was overblown. After all, he was just being friendly. "I work at a not-for-profit, so you know I don't have any money."

"Then how about something less tangible?" Jake leaned against the bar, resting one elbow casually on the flat surface.

"I'm not retracting a claim over a swizzle stick."

"Then how about dinner?"

The smile fell from Sarah's face. So much for her overblown worries. "Are you trying to get me fired?"

He looked visibly stunned by her question. "Fired? For what?"

"Cavorting with the enemy." He couldn't be that thick, could he?

"Dinner is hardly 'cavorting.' "

"Isn't it? Besides, every time I so much as see you in person, my boss appears or reads about it in the trades."

"The trades?" He puffed up his chest in mock importance. "I know I have a reputation in town, but I didn't think it was *that* impressive."

"It isn't. But a picture of us jaunting down the red carpet at the *Lusitania* premiere ended up in *The Hollywood Reporter*."

"Somehow I find that hard to believe."

"Okay, it wasn't a picture of us. It was a picture of Rick Daniels. We just happened to be in it."

"Were we kissing?"

"What?" Sarah looked around, expecting Bonnie to reappear at any moment.

"Were we kissing?" he repeated slowly, as if to a witness on the stand. "Were we doing anything to suggest something other than a completely professional relationship?"

Sarah folded her arms across her chest, annoyed by his cavalier attitude. "You were whispering to me."

He snitched a cherry from the bar, pulling it off the stem with his teeth. "I see how that could be mistaken for an intimate relationship. How did you explain it?"

"I said my roommate who works at the studio got the tickets and was standing just out of frame."

"Good thinking. Plausible, difficult to disprove. Quite a convenient alibi."

"And one I don't want to use again," Sarah shot back, frustrated with his inability to grasp the seriousness of the situation.

He tossed the cherry stem onto the bar. "I've been dealing with Bonnie Weston for a few years now. She's fair, rational, and not likely to fire you based on some pretty inconclusive evidence."

"I don't want *any* evidence," Sarah insisted, the end of the swizzle stick digging into her palm.

"Then come to dinner with me. We can even talk about claims if you'd like. Give it the veneer of respectability."

Sarah stepped close to Jake, pinning him with a hard look, all of her humor gone. "Listen, I don't know what kind of game you're playing, but I'm not playing along."

He opened his mouth to protest, but Sarah held up a menacing finger to silence him.

"You may have all your family money to fall back on, but some of us have to work for a living."

"I work," he replied, his eyes narrowing in anger, but Sarah wasn't about to back down. It was time to put an end to this, even if it meant wounding his overdeveloped pride.

"Obviously not hard enough, or you'd understand the importance of keeping a job." She poked an angry finger into his chest, the glittery swizzle stick glinting under the halogen lights. "So stop trying to wreck my career with your frat-boy flirting."

Sarah turned on her heel and stormed out of the bar before Jake could reply. As she jammed the elevator call button, she struggled to stop her hands from trembling. Those were serious accusations to throw at an opposing counsel whose cooperation she needed to get her job done. Was she overreacting? Had she read his signals wrong? If the studios talked to one another about how to interpret the Basic Agreement to their advantage, they probably talked to one another about the MAG attorneys too. She could only imagine what he'd tell the other studios about her.

The elevator doors opened, and she quickly stepped in, breathing a sigh of relief when they slid closed without anyone else joining her. She wasn't overreacting. His signals were as clear as the residuals language Lion Studios chose to violate. Let Jake say what he wanted; she'd rather get into trouble for telling him off than get fired for entertaining his inappropriate advances. So why didn't she feel triumphant? Why did she feel like she'd made a big mistake? Despite a desire to ignore it, she felt a little weak where Jake was concerned. No, she wasn't weak, only susceptible to the dazzling charms of Hollywood. She'd avoided his advances once before; she could easily do it again.

Storming through the hotel lobby and out to the curb, she handed her ticket to the parking valet. The cool evening air was a welcome relief, but standing there waiting for her car was torture. All around her people were leaving the party, laughing as they said good-bye. What she wouldn't give to be in such a good mood. Finally, the valet drove up in her Sentra. After slipping the man a tip, she jumped inside, flipped on the CD player, and pulled out into traffic.

The loud music thumping through the speakers did nothing to clear her mind. Instead, a hundred thoughts, including some that made her blush, fought to be heard. What was she doing thinking about Jake? She'd never been the type to fall for a smooth-talking man. No, she much preferred men like David, who decided to disappoint her just when she needed his support the most. Letting out a deep sigh, she turned off the freeway toward home.

Resisting the urge to head for the beach, she turned down the music as she drove into her neighborhood. After pulling into the parking garage, she killed the engine, sitting alone in the quiet concrete structure for a few minutes. Maybe she was letting her imagination get away from her. After all, recovering from David, combined with the prospect of spending her first holiday alone in a new city away from all her family and friends, was enough to leave a girl a little emotional. No wonder she was seeing things that didn't exist.

Maybe I should go home for Christmas, she thought. However, with the holiday less than a month away, the chances of getting a flight at a reasonable price were pretty slim. She thought about calling one of her friends to vent, but with the three-hour time difference, they'd kill her for waking them. If they didn't kill her, they might listen sympathetically, but what could they offer in the way of advice? They were all married with kids, and very few of them still worked.

Suddenly, her big new life in LA didn't feel so great. What was the point of having success if there was no one to share it with? Perhaps she'd imagined Jake flirting with her because she wanted to believe that another man, especially a successful one, might be interested in her. Normally, she'd unload on Dinah, but she hated to call her when she was traveling for work. Not wanting to feel even more pathetic by having a pity party in her car, Sarah got out and made her way toward the stairs, suddenly feeling very alone.

Jake slammed the Porsche into gear, tearing down the freeway toward home. The image of Sarah disappearing around the corner without so much as a second look continued to plague him. No opposing counsel from any of the entertainment unions had ever had the nerve to talk to him that way. Granted, he'd crossed a few lines, but no lawyer, no woman, had ever taken offense before.

Guiding his Porsche off the freeway, he steered the car down the hill toward Pacific Coast Highway instead of turning right toward home. He needed time to think and to develop a new strategy before he turned Sarah off completely. At a stoplight, he put down the convertible top, deeply inhaling the sticky sea air. Though he found certain aspects of LA boring at times, it could still impress him with the allure of an open road following the shore. When the light turned green, he stepped on the gas, sending the car shooting down the winding road, deftly responding to his control of the wheel and the clutch. If only women were as simple as cars, as quick to rev up and as easy to steer.

He laughed to himself, realizing a woman as easy to control as his car no longer interested him. Wasn't it Sarah's ability to stand up to him and hold her own that appealed to him? What woman had the same fire in her eyes as Sarah did when she spoke to him? He respected her more than all the women he'd dated who were so afraid of offending him, they wouldn't even complain if their food was cold or their feet hurt. Such slavish devotion might have appealed to him when he was the newest hot young lawyer in town. Now he hated it. Luckily, Sarah Steele was no doormat.

Jake downshifted into a sharp corner, his headlights catching the white foam of the surf before turning back onto the road. The wind whipped his hair around, growing cooler the farther north he drove. He welcomed the cold. It helped him concentrate on forming a plan and kept his mind from wandering to Sarah's infectious laugh and lively eyes.

He slammed a hand against the steering wheel in frustration. She'd turned him down again. He was obsessed with a woman who'd shut him down hard. He couldn't leave things the way they were. He needed her.

Only for the arbitration, he reminded himself, though he knew it was a lie. He'd never won by cheating, and he wasn't about to start now. As he drove past the Malibu mansions to where the road opened up toward Point Mugu, an idea hit him. Relationships were about negotiations, and the best negotiations involved compromise. Somewhere in all this was a compromise; all he had to do was find it. The hard part would be getting Sarah to sign off on the deal.

Chapter Six

Sarah sat in her office, finally relaxing after days of jumping every time the intercom buzzer sounded or Bonnie walked by. All day last Friday she'd expected Bonnie to storm in and ream her out for being rude to someone as important as Jake Rappaport. Hadn't she specifically asked Sarah to be friendly with him in an effort to resolve claims? Instead of being friendly, Sarah had poked him in the chest and called him a frat boy. She didn't think someone like Jake would let such an insult go unchecked. If he didn't call to complain about Sarah's accusations, surely he'd call about her very unprofessional finger-poking. Though it seemed out of character for Jake to run to a superior over a little misunderstanding, she knew he must be looking for any angle to help him win the upcoming arbitration. Complaining to Bonnie about her wild accusations and insisting she remove Sarah from the case was certainly one such angle. However, Friday had ended without the anticipated reprimand or the expected chewing out ever materializing.

Over the weekend, Sarah enjoyed a break from worrying.

Dinah, returned from her trip, took her shopping, helping her choose a few new LA-appropriate outfits. Afterward, they spent the afternoon at a spa, indulging in massages and manicures. It felt great to enjoy being a woman with a friend who understood what it was like to be successful and still single.

Though Sarah reluctantly greeted Monday, work proved busy, making the days fly by. Now, with Thursday quickly drawing to a close, she knew the imagined tongue-lashing would never come. Toward the end of the day, she even began to think her little blowup had put Jake in his place. She'd e-mailed and faxed his office with a number of responses to demands, even sending a few new demands of her own along for fun. However, the only person to call her from Lion Studios was Steve Manning. Perhaps Jake had lost interest in her, moved on to some easy intern with a thirst for well-connected men. Although the thought should have made her happy, on some level it bothered her.

The intercom buzzed, interrupting her musing.

"Yes?" Sarah answered, admiring her metallic pink nail polish while she typed up an e-mail to Raven Productions.

"Jake Rappaport is on your line." Her secretary rushed the words, obviously afraid to keep him on hold any longer than necessary.

Sarah's fingers stopped typing midsentence, her hands poised over the keyboard. She looked at the flashing button on her line. *Rats.* Why couldn't he have waited until Monday? She almost told her secretary to say she wasn't in, then changed her mind. He was probably calling about a claim. It was silly to go on thinking there was more to it than work.

"I'll take it," Sarah answered, hearing the secretary let

out a small sigh of relief. Taking a deep breath, she pushed the button on her phone. "This is Sarah."

"Sarah." No pleasantries, just business. That was a good sign. "I have your demand for *Gangway* in front of me. I think we should settle."

Sarah quickly shifted into business mode as they launched into a lengthy settlement discussion. He offered a reasonable amount, but she negotiated for a few hundred dollars more before they agreed to settle. As the business conversation wound down, she congratulated herself on acting professionally in front of Jake. However, he was quick to ruin her feeling of accomplishment.

"I haven't heard from you since I asked you to dinner last week. I was beginning to think that maybe you hadn't even enjoyed attending the premiere or the after party with me." His voice sent a small shiver up her spine, one she did her best to ignore.

"I did enjoy that, thank you. And you have heard from me. I faxed your office just this morning."

"You know what I mean," he replied, his voice smooth, too smooth. "How about dinner tonight? I have a meeting near your office, and there's a great sushi place not far from there. We can discuss a couple of other claims."

She hesitated, stunned. The man was either persistent or dense. "I think our discussion of last Thursday night should serve as a sufficient answer to your inquiry."

Jake offered a throaty chuckle in reply. "You leveled some pretty heavy accusations at me."

"You didn't deny them."

"I didn't agree with them either. You have no proof of any inappropriate behavior."

"The proof is circumstantial."

"Your 'proof' consists of one business lunch and two industry events, one of which we both attended by coincidence. Weak evidence, Miss Steele."

"The aforementioned dinner invitation serves to strengthen my circumstantial case, Mr. Rappaport."

"I didn't invite you to dinner for personal reasons. I suggested we discuss claims."

"A clever cover."

"For what?"

Sara felt herself mentally stumble. What could she say? She couldn't accuse him of being interested in her. Even if that was true, he was correct—all the evidence was circumstantial. To say it aloud would make her look like an idiot, especially if she were wrong. However, she felt there was more to all his attention than just an interest in discussing claims in person. *Feelings.* Didn't David always say that feelings were a female lawyer's weakness? He loved to believe that women argued with feelings, while men argued with logic. Not this time. No, Sarah would silence her feelings and let her logical mind do the talking.

"For trying to charm me into going soft on Lion Studios by settling a few claims for less-than-favorable terms for you."

"Then come to dinner. I'll show you how tough I can be," he challenged.

A million reasons why she should politely decline came to mind, but none of them escaped her mouth. If he wanted a challenge, especially a logical one, then she'd put her feelings aside and give him one. "All right. We'll meet and discuss a few claims. Besides, I haven't tried sushi yet. Why not do it on Lion's dime?"

"Great. I'm glad to hear you're willing to give sushi a roll." He laughed, and Sarah rolled her eyes, silently groaning at the pun. The easy familiarity between them made warning bells go off again, but he spoke before she could change her mind or redeem herself. "I'll see you at Sushi Catalina at six-thirty."

The line went dead. Sarah dropped her head into her hands and silently cursed herself for being so weak around Jake. She obviously hadn't been this weak in law school, so what was different now? She knew exactly what was different, though she hated to admit it. In law school life had seemed clear and full of direction. She'd had a boyfriend, a heavy class load, and well-defined career goals. Now, things all seemed very much up in the air, good week at work or not. Also, Dinah was in Las Vegas for the next couple of days for another press junket, leaving Sarah with only the TV for company tonight. She and Jake had just enjoyed a very professional conversation. What harm could there be in a dinner?

Jake looked across the table at Sarah, watching her eyes scan the menu and seeing confusion over what to order mingling with surprise at the prices.

"Don't worry. It's on me," he said, but it did little to smooth the delicate crease between her eyes.

"It seems like so much for something that's not even cooked."

He laughed, amazed again at her honesty. No other woman in LA would be so candid if she were being treated at the exclusive Sushi Catalina, yet to Sarah the place was just another overpriced restaurant.

He continued to watch her while she read the menu. She

wore a tasteful, light pink button-down blouse over nice black trousers. The outfit smacked of East Coast, providing a refreshing contrast to the usual Hollywood business-casual attire of "anything goes." Subtle makeup highlighted her features instead of trying to improve or correct them. Her hair fell about her face in soft waves, and when she tilted her head down to see the bottom of the menu, a strand fell across her face. Jake resisted the urge to reach across the table and tuck it behind her ear.

"Do you want me to recommend something for your first time?" he asked.

She laid down the menu with a mixture of relief and annoyance. "My 'first time'?" she objected.

"It is, isn't it?"

"Yes, but it sounds wrong when you say it."

"It's fun to be a little wrong sometimes, don't you think?" Jake leaned his elbows on the table, flashing a winning smile.

"Only when it comes to the *Tidal Wave* claim," she shot back, resting her elbows on the table in a no-nonsense position to challenge his.

Jake sat back, slightly checked. A small pile of files sat on the table next to her plate, indicating she was serious about keeping their dinner date professional. To maintain her attention, he knew he had to play along. After all, he didn't want another tongue-lashing like the one at Tiki Mai Tai. The bruise from where she'd poked him had only just disappeared.

Luckily the waiter appeared, saving him from her and himself. Jake ordered, explaining the ingredients in each roll and removing any from the list she objected to before the waiter left.

"If I ever leave LA, Sushi Catalina is the one restaurant I'll miss the most, especially their Sumo roll," Jake said, filling a small dish with soy sauce and mixing in a dab of wasabi.

"I don't picture you leaving LA. You seem very much at home here," she observed, finishing her sake.

"No need to get insulting." Jake laughed, refilling her small sake glass.

"You don't like LA?"

"I like LA, but I miss being close to my family, and I miss seasons."

"I don't miss the cold," Sarah said, "but I do miss my family."

"Do you think you'll ever go back to Richmond?"

"Someday. I don't know. It all depends on where life takes me. I never thought it'd bring me here." Her hand swept the room, a wistful look in her eyes, as if she still didn't believe she was here or if she even wanted to be here.

"You don't plan your life?" He didn't know why that surprised him, but it did.

"I used to, but life refused to cooperate."

"You don't seem like the type of woman to give up."

"I didn't give up. I just changed my goals," she replied a little defensively, making him wonder what had happened to leave her with such a dim view of strategizing. "Do you plan?"

"Always."

"Does life always cooperate?"

"Of course."

"So you get everything you want?"

"Everything." He offered her a sly smile.

She sat back, folding her arms in disbelief. "No surprises, no disappointments?"

"Not usually."

"Must be very boring being you."

He fixed her with a pointed stare, noticing for the first time the flecks of gold in her hazel eyes. "Not at all. When I see something I want, I go after it. It's as simple as that."

She started a little, then held up her sake glass in salute. "I admire your fortitude."

He raised his glass, clinking it against hers before taking a sip. "So, what happened to make a woman like you give up on planning?"

She fiddled with her chopsticks, lining them up side by side next to her plate. "You don't want to know."

"I do."

"Well, I don't feel like telling you," she snapped.

He knew better than to push. Whatever it was, he wanted to take her into his arms, kiss away the worry crease between her eyes, and make her forget whatever gave her such a tentative look, as if coming to Los Angeles was still an agonizing decision.

"Look on the bright side. If you hadn't come to LA, we wouldn't have become friends."

She shot him a puzzled look that softened into a sassy smile. "I wouldn't call us *friends*."

"Colleagues, then," he offered in compromise.

"Colleagues." She raised her glass and clinked it against his. Their fingers gently brushed in the quick movement, leaving Jake with a delicious hint of her delicate, warm skin. She must have felt it too, for she hastily retracted her hand. To Jake's relief, the waiter brought out their order, and her easy mood returned.

Sarah proved to be an adventurous eater, willing to take

a chance on everything he gave her to try. He was careful to start her off easy with a California roll before introducing her to more adventurous combinations. Sushi, like other LA habits, had become second nature to him, almost routine. Seeing it through her eyes gave him the same new appreciation for the delicacy as it had for the premiere.

As the evening progressed, he ordered more dishes. While they ate, Jake was careful to discuss the claims and engage in debates concerning the sections of the Basic Agreement involved. He even settled a couple of minor claims in order to give the pretext of a business dinner. After a while, he gently guided the conversation away from work to the familiar topic of Virginia. Discussing home relaxed her more than the sake, allowing him to pepper her with innocuous questions simply to keep her talking. He enjoyed listening to her sweet voice and watching the light of the neon signs over the sushi bar glisten in her eyes. Steve would laugh if he saw him acting like some romantic idiot, but Jake didn't care. Steve wasn't here.

After dinner, Jake paid the bill, then escorted Sarah outside. They handed their tickets to the parking attendants, who hurried off to retrieve their cars.

"Now, that wasn't so bad, was it?" Jake asked.

"No. Sushi is better than I expected."

"I meant dinner with opposing counsel."

"Ah," she replied. "No, it wasn't so bad, though I don't think we should make it a habit."

"Too bad. You're an excellent debater. I know I pose a bit of a professional dilemma to you, but surely we can be friends."

Her smile dropped a little. "No, we can't. Bonnie wants

me to be friendly with you, but I don't think she'd like it if we were really friends."

"I happen to know for a fact that Bonnie Weston is good friends with a couple of in-house attorneys at Mountain Pictures. They worked together a few years ago. It's something you'll discover about Hollywood. Everyone is friends with everyone else because they've all worked together at one time or another."

"We never worked together."

"No, but we went to school together. It's practically the same thing."

"Practically, but not quite."

"Then there's no reason for us not to be friends."

He posed his response as a statement instead of a question, halting her ability to refuse his request. Luckily, the valets arrived with their cars before she could answer. He opened her car door, tipping the valet and holding up his hand to stop her from protesting.

"Thanks again," she said, slipping into the driver's seat and pulling the door closed. She rolled down the window to say something, but he didn't give her the chance.

"We'll talk again," he said quickly before taking his key from the attendant and getting into his own car. Watching her drive out of the parking lot, he knew he'd won a great victory. It was only a matter of time before he won the war.

Chapter Seven

Sarah jogged along the cliff-top path in Santa Monica, the Pacific Ocean spreading out to her right, glittering in the late-afternoon sun. Surfers bobbed in the waves, while scattered beach towels and umbrellas dotted the wide, sandy beach. She loved the warm, fall weather, knowing she'd never be able to do this in Richmond. She even considered taking a dip in the condo pool when she got home, assuming she could find her bathing suit. Today, however, despite the excitement of jogging so close to the beach in December, she still couldn't clear her mind.

She hadn't heard from Jake since their dinner Thursday night. Her rational mind told her to be thankful, but the irrational part of her couldn't stop chewing on it. Despite their having what she considered a great evening, Friday had passed without one e-mail or phone call. There wasn't even a fax from his office or any other indication he was thinking about her. She should have breathed a sigh of relief, but instead the silence made her anxious. Obviously, despite a good dinner and excellent conversation, he found her easy to dismiss. The idea irritated her, making her wonder when she'd stop acting like a schoolgirl and start acting like a grown woman.

She picked up her pace, her shoes falling hard on the asphalt path as it wound its way through palm trees and modern-art sculptures. In the distance, the large Ferris wheel turned lazily over the Santa Monica pier, while excited shouts from tourists on the mini roller-coaster mixed with the call of seagulls on the breeze. The sound of another jogger coming up behind her caught her attention, and she moved to the side to let him pass. Instead of passing, the jogger fell into step next to her.

"Hello, stranger," a rich male voice greeted her.

Sarah stumbled a little before regaining her stride.

"Jake, what are you doing here?" The question came out more harshly than she had intended, but he didn't seem to notice.

"I stopped by your place to see if you wanted to get coffee, and your roommate told me you were out jogging."

"She told you I was here?" Sarah asked, surprised. However, knowing how eager Dinah was to see her find a man, she wasn't totally shocked.

"Well, it took a little cajoling to get her to tell me, but in the end, as you can see, I won her over with my charm. I figured since I hadn't hit the gym today, I'd head out for a jog too and see if I could catch up with you."

"Why didn't you just call me on my cell?"

"I did, but according to Dinah, it just rang on the charger in your bedroom."

"Oh, yeah, I forgot it," Sarah mumbled. Actually, she'd left it behind on purpose, wanting to get away from everything for a little while. Who knew that part of the "everything" she was trying to get away from would track her down with Dinah's help? She made a mental note to talk to Dinah about it when she got home.

"Mind if I join you?" Jake asked, motioning down the jogging path.

Yes, Sarah thought but stopped the word from slipping out of her mouth. They were colleagues, old schoolmates, *friends.* She couldn't be unfriendly.

"Not at all." She smiled with false enthusiasm. She'd come here to clear her mind, and he was only cluttering it more.

"You never told me your real reason for coming to California," he said, the statement coming out hard and breathy as he ran.

Sarah struggled not to stumble over her surprise. "Why do you want to know?"

"Why won't you tell me? Is it juicy? Does it involve a scandal?"

"Hardly." Sarah laughed. "It's pretty boring."

"Why don't you tell me and let me decide?"

"Let's walk, then. I haven't got the breath to talk about it and jog."

"All right, we'll walk." He stopped dead, causing her to jog slightly ahead.

Stopping, she turned to take him in as she walked slowly back. He wore shorts, showing off muscular legs honed from jogging. A T-shirt advertising a past Lion Studios' release hung off his wide shoulders and clung to his slightly sweaty chest.

Why, in heaven's name, did I agree to tell him about myself? she thought. She could have given him a pat answer and continued jogging. Between keeping pace and breathing, there wouldn't have been much opportunity for any real conversation. Now she had to entertain him with her sad tale, of all things.

"Are you sure you want to hear it?"

"I love a good sob story," he teased, the fine lines at the corners of his eyes crinkling with his smile. A studio baseball cap covered his hair and, combined with his smile, gave him a boyish look.

"It's not exactly a sob story." This was wrong on so many levels, but her feet kept moving toward him.

"Let me guess. Small-town girl came to conquer the big city?"

"Richmond is hardly a small town." She tried to concentrate on her surroundings, attempting to ignore the spicy, sweaty smell of him as he walked beside her.

"All right, then your real dream is to be a screenwriter, and you're only working as a lawyer until you hit your big break."

"Pure fiction."

"It's pretty common in this town."

"Is that your story?" she asked, hoping he might forget about her history and concentrate on himself.

"Not at all. So tell me, what's the real story behind your big move?"

Darn. There was no putting him off. But how much should she tell him? He knew she was from back East and where she'd gone to law school. There was nothing left to distract him from the truth. But what harm was there in telling him? Surely she wasn't the first woman to move across the country for a new life. Besides, she could tell him the truth without telling him the whole truth.

"I wanted to see a little more of the world, experience a different city, do something unique. Richmond is nice, but it isn't LA."

"And there are no ex-boyfriends or ex-husbands here," he stated bluntly.

Sarah stared at him in disbelief. "How did you know?"

"It's a common enough story. Come on, confess—which ex is it?"

"Ex-fiancé."

He let out a slow whistle. "Worse than I thought."

"Excuse me?"

"No reason to be ashamed. You're probably better off without the jerk."

"You don't know the half of it," Sarah answered before thinking. She saw the glimmer of mirth in Jake's blue eyes and knew she'd fallen right into his trap. This was dangerous territory, bordering too much on genuine friendship. What she wouldn't give right now for one of the piles of claims on her desk—anything to keep him from getting too close.

"So, tell me all about it."

Sarah shrugged. "What's there to tell? I was a success, and he wasn't. He couldn't stand it."

"So he tried to hold you back. When he knew he couldn't, he cheated on you."

Sarah stopped dead, her mouth falling open in surprise. "What did you do, pump Dinah for information?"

"No," Jake replied, his eyes too sympathetic for Sarah's taste. "But I know men and women."

"I bet you do." Sarah narrowed her eyes in suggestive suspicion.

Jake threw up his hands in mock defense. "I don't know it from firsthand experience. I would never do that to a woman."

She wanted to call him a liar, but something in the way he said it made her believe him. He was too confident, too sure of himself and his success to stoop to David's level.

"No, I don't think you would."

"You'd better believe it. So, what happened?"

Sarah studied Jake, the warm look in his eyes surprising her. Gone was the overconfident fraternity-boy smirk she'd seen at lunch and at the premiere. Instead he took her in with genuine concern, as though her answer mattered. Sarah wondered if this was his latest attempt to coax *Tidal Wave* secrets out of her. However, the tenderness in his eyes, the understanding look on his face as he waited for her to answer told her it wasn't. A comfortable feeling spread through her, replacing some of her anxiety and making her feel that she could tell him anything.

Sarah started walking, needing the activity to build up her courage. Jake walked next to her, patiently waiting for her answer. "At one point maybe we were equals—you know, when we first met—but he wasn't as driven as I was. I thought he was, but he wasn't."

"What kind of law does he practice?"

"Personal injury."

"Slip-and-fall, huh?"

"Yeah, but I'm the fool who slipped and fell for him."

"He was probably so charming, you can hardly blame yourself."

"You're saying I'm a sucker for a charmer?"

He leaned in close, nudging her with his elbow. "No, or I'd have succeeded with you two weeks ago."

"Succeeded with me?" Again he seemed to be flirting, but she cautiously didn't press the matter. The possibility of being wrong about his intentions a second time was more than she could handle.

"Succeeded in getting you to drop the *Tidal Wave* claim," he clarified.

Sarah laughed. "You'd have to succeed with more people than me."

"I'm up for the challenge. So, what finally broke the camel's back with your ex?"

Sarah sighed. "I won my first big case."

"Taylor Manufacturing versus Richmond Workers Union."

A sinking feeling gripped her. Why did everyone always associate her with that case? There were others, ones she'd rather brag about than Taylor. "You've been reading about me?"

"Google—the best invention ever."

Sarah shook her head, simultaneously annoyed and flattered. Annoyed because he expected her to discuss the case. Flattered to know he'd been thinking about her. "I spent a lot of time on the case. David was really supportive at first, when it looked like I didn't have a chance of winning. Everything changed once the case picked up momentum. He was withdrawn and sulky, picking fights over nothing, canceling dates. At the time I was too busy to think about it. He wasn't even there the night the verdict came in."

"He was with someone else?" Jake asked gently, and Sarah nodded.

"His new secretary. I walked in on them. A few days after that, Dinah told me about the job at MAG. I applied, took the California Bar, and here I am."

"In Hollyweird."

"Exactly."

They ambled along the path together without speaking. The constant roar of engines rushing by on the street punctuated by the sound of crashing waves carried on the breeze filled the comfortable silence between them. However, Sarah's worries over the Taylor case refused to keep quiet.

"The thing is," Sarah continued, though she wasn't sure why, "the Taylor case was hardly worth getting upset over."

"You won a major victory."

"I won on a technicality—not a legal argument or a persuasive case but a technicality."

"That's not true. You successfully argued for the technicality to be applied, which opened the door for you to win the case based on your arguments."

"It was a weak strategy to win on."

Jake stopped, turning to face her. "What does it matter how you won as long as you won?"

"Is winning all that matters?"

"When it's important, yes. I read the details of the case. Taylor Manufacturing was wrong. What they were doing to their workers was wrong."

"You aren't going soft on labor, are you?" Sarah teased, trying to lighten the mood.

"No, but I can appreciate a real victory. You helped a lot of people."

"I got lucky. Now MAG expects me to win major arbitrations on behalf of its members. There won't always be technicalities."

"It wasn't a technicality. Taylor failed to file the paperwork on time. It was their responsibility to know the deadlines and procedures, and they didn't. You discovered it and used it to your advantage. A smart lawyer knows how to look for and use advantages, no matter how small. Don't sell yourself short."

Sarah took a deep breath, enjoying the encouragement. She'd always been afraid to highlight the truth behind her victory, afraid people would look down on her or call her a fraud, or worse. Instead, Jake knew the truth, and he was still impressed by her ability to argue the law, no matter how minor the point she'd decided to argue.

Jake stood in front of her, his eyes soft, supportive, and, most important, understanding. "You're a great lawyer. Don't ever think you aren't, and don't let anyone make you believe differently."

A strand of hair escaped her loose ponytail and fell across her face. He reached up, pushing it back behind her ear. His eyes never left hers, and his hand lingered a moment beside her cheek before he withdrew it. He continued to study her face, his body close, the spicy scent of his cologne hovering between them. Sarah wanted to touch him, to run her fingers over the strong line of his jaw and feel the shadowing stubble on his chin. A cool breeze wound past them, and she resisted the urge to step closer and wrap her arms around his narrow waist. She admired the strength of him, wanted to feel it and allow it to drive away her own doubts. As if reading her thoughts, he stepped closer, his head tilted toward hers. Despite her better judgment she leaned toward him, her head tilted up, her lips eagerly anticipating the soft feel of his.

Suddenly Jake's BlackBerry rang, breaking the spell. He stepped back, muttering a curse under his breath as he snatched it from the clip on his waistband and looked at the number. Instantly, the irritated look on his face vanished, replaced by a smile.

"Excuse me. I have to take this." He stepped off to one side, out of earshot.

She watched him chat, unable to catch more than a few words of the conversation over the traffic noise. It was obviously a personal call, one important enough to interrupt the moment. Sarah felt a slight blush creeping into her cheeks as she realized just how close she'd come to kissing him and stepping over the worst possible professional boundary she could cross. She wasn't even stepping—she was throwing herself across it.

Something in the conversation made Jake laugh. Sarah frowned, wondering if he was talking to a woman. The feeling surprised her. She couldn't be jealous, could she? No, it was impossible. The desire to jog off while he was distracted overwhelmed her, but she stayed put. Judging by his previous behavior, he would probably follow her and demand some excuse for why she'd literally run off. If she felt embarrassed now, she'd definitely feel embarrassed then. No, it was better to wait. Once he was off the phone, she'd act as if nothing had almost happened between them.

Needing something else to focus on, she yanked the band out of her ponytail and shook out her hair. Running her fingers through the thick waves, she looked up to see Jake watching her, a strange look of longing on his face.

Advantage. The word flashed through her mind like a warning. Hadn't he said a good lawyer knows how to use advantages, no matter how small? She'd almost fallen for his caring-friend routine—hard enough to risk making a fool out of herself in the middle of Santa Monica and handing him a major advantage. But what about the heated look in his eyes? No, it wasn't there. It was just a temporary delusion brought on by all her old feelings about David. Turning away from Jake and toward the ocean, she quickly pulled her hair back into a ponytail, struggling with shaking hands to secure it with the band.

"Sorry about that," Jake said, coming to stand next to her. "My brother and his wife are driving up from San Diego. He's out here for a legal conference, and they're flying back to Virginia Monday morning."

"It must be interesting being from a family of lawyers. I bet holiday discussions are a lot of fun," Sarah joked, relieved to learn he hadn't been talking to another woman. What was wrong with her? Her thoughts were as erratic as a lovesick teenage girl's.

"Yeah, sometimes we really get into it." Jake laughed. "Except for my sister."

"She doesn't like arguing during the holidays?"

"No, she's a pediatrician. That's considered a rebel in my family."

"Impressive. Thanks for walking with me, but I need to go. I have things to do," Sarah mumbled, silently cursing herself. For a lawyer, her brain refused to respond quickly today.

"Me too. Let's grab coffee tomorrow afternoon, and we'll continue this conversation. Three o'clock at the Coffee Pot?"

"Uh, well . . ." *Come on, girl, think of an excuse,* her mind yelled, but only stammers came out.

"Great. I'll see you tomorrow at three." Jake jogged off before Sarah had a chance to refuse. Silently she cursed herself for being so weak. How hard would it have been to say no or come up with some excuse? Even if her brain did turn to mush around Jake, this had to stop, and it had to stop now.

Jake sat across the table from his brother and sister-in-law, slowly swirling the olive in his martini. Despite the adult drink and surroundings, his brother, Derrick, was doing his best to make Jake feel like a kid tonight. It was all Jake could do to remain seated and finish out the dinner with even a modicum of politeness.

"Come on, bro, are you going to spend your whole life living in the fast lane?"

"You mean being successful?" Jake growled, staring hard at his brother in disbelief.

"Are you really happy here?"

"Would I be here if I wasn't?"

"Yeah, if only to prove us all wrong."

Jake took a sip of his drink, resisting the urge to toss it back in one smooth motion and order another, perhaps two.

"Don't you want more from life?" Derrick continued, ignoring the irritated way Jake drummed his fingers on the table. "You haven't dated anyone since Jill."

"I've dated lots of people since Jill."

"Don't you want more than flings with starlets?"

"Derrick!" his wife, Maggie, chastised.

"Sorry." He patted her hand lovingly before turning his attention back to Jake.

"Derrick, why don't you call and see how Megan is doing?" Maggie suggested before Derrick could say anything else.

"She's fine," Derrick replied.

Maggie pinned him with a stern look. "Go call."

Finally picking up on his wife's not-too-subtle hint, he grabbed his cell phone and rose. "Okay, I'll call, but I'll be right back."

"I can hardly wait," Jake mumbled as Derrick made his way toward the front of the restaurant.

Maggie turned to Jake, offering him a sympathetic smile. "Don't be mad. He's only giving you a hard time because he cares about you."

"I know, but it doesn't make it any less irritating."

Maggie took a sip of her drink, then fixed Jake with a serious look. "I've heard your dad is thinking of opening an LA office."

"So I've heard. I'm pretty well settled at Lion."

"But you didn't say 'happy.'"

He leaned back against the booth, placing his arms along the top. One thing Jake admired about Maggie was the way she went straight to the heart of an issue without beating a person over the head with it. Her delicate approach cut faster and deeper than she realized and was far more effective than his brother's jackhammer method. "Why didn't *you* become an attorney?"

Maggie laughed. "No thanks. There are enough attorneys in this family already."

Before Jake could answer, Derrick returned.

"Have you talked any sense into him?" he asked, offering Maggie a quick, affectionate kiss. Jake felt a momentary pang of jealousy but quickly shook it off.

"I don't know." Maggie turned to Jake. "Have I?"

Jake examined them, noticing the eager way they waited for his response. He felt his parents' hands in this conversation. He knew Dad wanted him to join the family firm, and Mom, well, Jake was the last unmarried son, so he could easily guess her concern.

"I'm very happy," he lied. Though his brother and sister-in-law nodded, he could tell from their eyes that they didn't believe him.

"So where's Megan?" Jake asked, desperate to change the subject.

"A friend of mine from college—Chuck Spalding, you remember him—has a little girl her age. He lives in the Palisades. Megan is enjoying movie night with them. Speaking of which, they're having a barbecue tomorrow. Why don't you come? Megan would love to see her favorite uncle."

"I can't. I have plans tomorrow afternoon. I'm meeting someone for coffee."

Both of their eyes lit up, and Jake knew he'd made a mistake mentioning the topic.

"A woman?" Maggie asked.

"Yes, but not a date. We went to law school together. She just moved here from Richmond. She's an attorney for the Movie Actors Guild."

"You're seeing someone who works in labor? I never thought I'd live to see the day." Derrick laughed.

"I'm not 'seeing' her."

"Good, then bring her along."

"So the two of you can cross-examine her as a potential date?"

"It would be a change from the starlet du jour you usually introduce when we visit. Besides, if you're not dating, there's no problem. Chuck knows lots of people in the business. It could benefit both of you to meet him."

"I'll think about it," Jake said, dreading the idea. Any woman he brought around Derrick and Maggie would immediately be scrutinized for her partner potential. Still, it would be nice to bring a woman who could hold a conversation. And if Sarah successfully networked, perhaps the whole conflict-of-interest issue might resolve itself, though there was no real reason to resolve it, since they were just friends.

Finishing the last of his martini, he motioned to the waiter for another. He hadn't been able to get Sarah out of his head for the last two weeks. He might lie to Derrick about his relationship with Sarah, but how much longer could he lie to himself? On the jogging path, he'd seen the wanting look in her eyes. It was the same look he knew had graced his own face when he watched her shake out her hair, the sunlight dancing off the water behind her. He'd spent the entire evening with the image seared into his mind, his lips aching for the kiss they'd almost enjoyed.

He'd also seen the fear in her eyes when she realized what they had almost done. No matter how he might try to justify it, a relationship with her was dangerous, and they both knew it. Still, he couldn't stay away or give her up, not just yet. All he needed to do was maintain their friendship until the arbitration was over.

Chapter Eight

A barbecue with his family?" Dinah asked, sitting on Sarah's bed and watching her dig through her jewelry box. "Men don't usually introduce women they've just met to their family if they aren't serious about them."

"It's not like that." Sarah wrapped an onyx necklace around her neck, struggling to fasten the lobster-claw clasp.

"Let me rephrase that. Men like Jake don't introduce women they've just met to their family."

"It's not like that," Sarah insisted, examining her outfit one more time in the closet-door mirror. *Conservative* was the word for the day. She didn't want to give Jake's family or any of the other guests the impression that they were dating or interested in each other. When he'd called to ask her to the event, she'd hesitated. Overnight she'd come up with a hundred reasons why they shouldn't have coffee, but not one of them came to mind when he asked her to the barbecue. Perhaps it was the way he'd phrased it, making it sound like an industry event where they could network. It seemed less intimate and personal than coffee—until he'd mentioned the part about his family right before hanging up.

"Who knows? Maybe his brother is single, and he wants to introduce us," Sarah suggested.

"Right, and pigs are flying." Dinah rolled her eyes. "Come on, Sarah, you aren't this naïve."

Sarah stopped fussing with her clothes, meeting Dinah's eyes in the mirror. "No, I'm not naïve, but Jake is the first guy I've met who doesn't try to compete with me. He actually listens when I'm making a point, and he enjoys debating me."

" 'Debating' you?" Dinah asked with questioning disbelief. "Is that what it's called now?"

"All right, I know it sounds strange, but it's true. I feel like I can be myself around him. He wants to be friends, so why not enjoy his friendship?"

"Because you've fallen for him."

"I haven't fallen for him," Sarah protested with less than stellar conviction.

"Then stop now before it's too late," Dinah replied with enough severity to stun Sarah.

"Wait, wasn't this the woman who encouraged me to go to the premiere with him, then told him where to find me yesterday?"

"I didn't think you two were serious."

"There is no 'you two,' and we aren't serious. I'm not even his type."

"You're breathing. From what I hear, that's his type."

"Starlets are his type, not lawyers. Besides, what harm can there be in spending a small amount of time with him?"

"The loss of your job, your professional reputation, your big new life in LA."

Sarah looked away, smoothing her hands over her khaki pants before pulling the wrinkles out of her black knit top. Thinking of the near kiss on the jogging path, she knew Dinah was right. Despite her constant insistence on friendship, she wanted more, but she also knew she couldn't have it. No matter what she might feel for Jake, she couldn't compete with other LA women for his attention. So why not enjoy the way his friendship made her feel? "We're just friends."

"Men like Jake don't have female friends, and women like you don't have male friends."

"Well, maybe it's time for me to learn how to be friends with a man without falling for him." In the abstract it seemed like an easy thing to do, but the reality had her stumped. Once again she felt as if her life was being turned upside down by a man. But she wouldn't let it happen this time. She'd conquer this weakness. She had to.

"It's a good skill to learn, but not with Jake." Dinah shook her head, her serious look fading to one of cautious humor. "You have to start out small—you know, like Brad down the hall. No chance of falling for him after one or two dates."

"True. I've seen him in his swim trunks. No danger there." Sarah laughed, breaking the tense mood. "Or perhaps the security guard at Lion Studios?"

Dinah thought for a moment, her usual humor back in full force. "He'd be a good one to start with. Have you seen his biceps?"

Sarah nodded. "He made sure I saw them when I checked in."

"Of course it's not really the guard's biceps you're interested in."

"Isn't it?"

"Of course not. It's his brain." Dinah and Sarah broke into a fit of laughter, and for a moment Sarah felt her worry disappear.

Suddenly, the doorbell rang, and all relaxed feelings quickly vanished. They both stopped laughing as they exchanged serious looks.

"I guess you'd better answer it," Dinah said.

Sarah hesitated, looking between her friend and the front door.

"Wish me luck?" she asked in the most lighthearted voice she could muster.

Dinah offered her a wicked, knowing smile. "You aren't on a date. No need for luck."

"Funny," Sarah tossed over her shoulder as she walked to the living room, Dinah following at a discreet distance.

Pulling open the front door, Sarah resisted the urge to suck in her breath in amazement. Jake wore a fitted polo shirt, highlighting his muscles like a character's from a British spy movie. His brown hair dipped across his forehead in a casual way she hadn't seen before. If she'd been in danger of kissing him on the jogging path when he was dressed in a sweaty T-shirt, she'd be lucky to get through today without throwing herself at him. Dinah was right about the danger, but Sarah couldn't back out now.

"Ready to go?" she asked, careful to keep any hint of passion or attraction out of her voice.

"I'm always ready," he said with a smirk, making the butterflies in her stomach flutter.

"Then let's go." She strolled out the door past him, ignoring the comment, and he followed. Jake stepped back as Sarah turned to close the door. She caught Dinah's eye, and her friend mouthed "Be careful" before Sarah shut the door.

A few clouds dotted the blue sky, and the low autumn sun cut across everything with a brilliant, clear light, creating crisp shadows and enhancing the color of the pool, the plants, and the trees. The Santa Ana winds from the night before had cleared the air, providing everyone on the second story with a clear view of the Santa Monica Mountains. They walked downstairs, through the courtyard, and out the iron gate in silence. Approaching his Porsche, Jake jogged forward to open the passenger door.

"Nice car," Sarah remarked, slipping into the leather racing seat. He closed the door, then walked around to his side, giving her a moment to take in the masculine interior. It was a car built to convey confidence and power, and the manly dashboard with its carbon-fiber trim and leather-capped gearshift suited Jake.

The driver's-side door opened, and Jake hopped in, firing up the car with the push of a button.

"Top down?" he asked.

"Sounds great."

He pushed another button, and the roof retracted. "Let's go."

He stepped on the gas, shifting the car into gear and pulling out into traffic. It felt great to speed along Sunset Boulevard next to Jake. Sarah leaned back against the high seat, closing her eyes and allowing the cool afternoon air to wash over her. What would it be like to drive with him every weekend, exploring the small beach communities scattered along the coast? She imagined the two of them having quiet dinners together in little undiscovered cafés, watching the sunset sparkle off the ocean.

"Are you all right?" Jake asked, bringing the car to a halt at a stoplight.

Sarah snapped open her eyes. "Yes, I'm just enjoying the beautiful afternoon."

Thank goodness for dark sunglasses, she thought, afraid he would see the romantic notions in her eyes if she took them off.

The light turned green before he had a chance to respond, and in a second Jake snapped the car into gear, racing off down the street. The roar of the engine, combined with the wind from the open top, made conversation difficult. It gave Sarah a chance to clear her mind while enjoying the excitement of speeding along the winding neighborhood roads.

The western stretch of Sunset Boulevard looked nothing like the flashy neon, club-lined Hollywood section of the strip. Here the road wound through tree-lined estates as it made its way toward the ocean. Taking in the dappled afternoon sunlight filtering through the pine trees of the Pacific Palisades, Sarah almost forgot she was in a city. For a moment she understood the glamour and allure of Los Angeles and why so many people wanted it. It felt great to drive in a convertible on a perfect sunny day in December.

"Where are we going?" she asked at the next stoplight.

"Will Rogers Park."

"Only in LA do they name parks after TV cowboys."

Jake's laugh matched the car's deep idle. "It used to be his ranch. His house is still there, but it's now part of a park and polo field."

Before Sarah could answer, the light turned green. Jake made a hard right off Sunset Boulevard onto a narrow road winding uphill through a neighborhood of old California ranch-style houses. They made the last turn, and the park came into view. The actor's old ranch house, nestled at the base of the small hill, overlooked a large, grassy expanse separated into two parts by a gravel parking area. On the left side of the parking lot was a picnic area with tables and cement barbecues. On the other side stood another grassy picnic area and the polo field. Polo players, dressed in their respective team colors, drove their sweat-covered mounts after the ball, the horses' hooves tearing up chunks of turf as they ran. A sizable crowd stood along the field's white fence, cheering as mallets swung toward the ball, changing the direction of play every few seconds.

Next to the polo field, the barbecue was in full swing, but it was unlike any barbecue she'd ever seen. She'd expected a casual affair, with the men manning the grills while the women hovered around tables covered with an assortment of salads. Instead, the catered affair sported tables covered with red-and-white checkered tablecloths and enormous amounts of food. Servers dressed like cowboys moved among the chatting guests, offering lemonade in jam jars. At the far edge of the picnic tables, next to the catering company van, a chef manned a large barbecue spewing hickory-scented smoke into the air. Just beyond the barbecue, a bouncy inflatable castle vibrated with the force of all the little kids jumping around inside while their bored nannies stood in a group chatting nearby. This was far from the intimate friends-and-family gathering she and Dinah had imagined, and Sarah felt a little silly for spending so much time worrying.

"Who's hosting this barbecue?" Sarah asked as Jake pulled into a parking space and killed the engine.

"A friend of my brother's. He's in the business and loves polo. There's a lot of people here you should talk to who could help your career."

"Great," Sarah replied with less enthusiasm than she felt. She should have breathed a sigh of relief. Instead she fought back a wave of disappointment. He'd invited her to an industry event in an effort to make contacts, not because he had any personal interest in her. Yet the whole way here she'd sat in his car enjoying fantasies of exciting weekend getaways. Luckily he knew nothing about her dreams or her conversation with Dinah. If he did, she'd feel more embarrassed than she already felt. Dinah was right. Jake liked women. He probably made them all feel special during their limited time spent together. Why should Sarah be any different? Putting on her best business face, she accompanied him across the parking lot toward the party.

"Uncle Jake!" A young girl broke from the bouncy-castle line and ran across the park toward him, her eyes wide with excitement. Much to Sarah's surprise, Jake dropped down to one knee, threw open his arms, and allowed the girl to hurl herself against his chest.

"How are you doing, Peanut?" he asked, standing and swinging her around, causing her to squeal with laughter.

"We went to Disneyland," she explained, wrapping her arms about his neck and planting a large kiss on his cheek.

"Really? What did you see and do there?"

The little girl chatted while Jake carried her back toward the waiting party. There was something touching about the way he held his niece, allowing her to hang on to his pristine polo shirt, her dirty shoes kicking at the sides of his well-pressed khakis.

Sarah walked alongside him, listening to the little girl describe Disneyland and noticing the way her eyes studied Sarah with a mix of interest and suspicion. She whispered into Jake's ear, eliciting a wide smile from Jake. He lowered her to the ground, took her by hand, and gently turned her toward Sarah.

"Megan, this is Sarah. Sarah, this is Megan."

"Nice to meet you," Megan replied, holding out her hand. Sarah took it, allowing her arm to be exuberantly shaken.

"Are you Uncle Jake's new girlfriend?" Megan asked. Leave it to a little kid to be so blunt.

Sarah felt the slight heat of a blush creeping into her cheeks. "No, your uncle and I are just friends."

Megan glanced up at her uncle, a curious look on her face.

"Go tell your dad we're here," Jake instructed before Megan could make further inquiries. She scrunched up her face with a confused expression.

"But Daddy already knows. He can't wait to meet your *friend*," she replied in a singsong voice, putting special emphasis on the word *friend*.

"Oh, really. Did he say that?"

"Yes." She stuck out her tongue at Jake, and he stuck out his tongue in return.

"I'll give you a quarter if you go tell him again."

"Okay." Megan held out her hand, expecting payment up front. Sarah laughed as Jake rolled his eyes in mock frustration, then produced the promised quarter. He dropped it into her open palm, and she skipped off across the grass yelling, "Dad, Uncle Jake is here with his *friend*."

The little girl's mother took her hand and chastised her for making so much noise, while Jake smiled apologetically at Sarah. "Little kids—you know how they are."

"Of course," Sarah replied, having spent more summers than she could remember either helping out in her mother's summer classes or working as a camp counselor. It was sweet to see a man of Jake's professional standing interact so easily with his niece.

"Come on, and I'll introduce you to Derrick." Jake placed his hand on the small of her back, guiding her off to the right. The warmth of his hand came through her thin sweater, and she had to stop herself from leaning into his sturdy chest.

Loud cheering drew her attention to the polo field, and Sarah turned in time to see one player send the ball sailing into the goal.

"Do you like polo?" Jake asked.

"I've never watched it before."

"Then you're in for a treat."

Sarah smiled as Jake led her toward his family. A man a couple of years older than Jake but sporting the same boyish grin and blue eyes quickly approached them.

"Sarah, may I introduce my older brother, Derrick?"

Derrick held out his hand, and Sarah shook it. "I'm always pleased to meet another lawyer, especially a friend of Jake's."

He too emphasized the word *friend* in a strange way, shooting his brother a suggestive glance. Sarah could only imagine what Jake had told his family about her. "I'm glad Jake decided to bring you along. We've heard a lot about you."

"Have you?" Sarah asked, casting a curious look in Jake's direction, a slight glimmer of hope flaring up in her mind.

"I've told him about your work at MAG," Jake explained with a shrug, quickly dampening Sarah's glimmer. At least he was making an effort to clarify the situation for her, even if her mind didn't want any clarification.

"Jake tells me you're from Virginia. My wife and I live in Virginia. Have you ever thought of moving back?"

"I just moved here, but who knows? Maybe in a year or two."

"Jake's thinking of joining the family firm. There's an opening coming up."

Sarah looked at Jake with a stunned, questioning glance. Obviously the comment surprised Jake too, because his eyes went wide before narrowing with his obviously forced smile.

"Derrick likes to joke." He clapped his brother on the back in a hard but playful way, his hand tightening in warning on his brother's shoulder. "He knows I'm not leaving Lion."

"Lion isn't the only place you can successfully practice law," Derrick insisted, visibly increasing Jake's irritation.

Luckily, a woman about Derrick's age quickly came up behind him, saving Sarah from witnessing any further sibling bickering.

"Derrick, stop causing trouble. You know Jake's not interested in the family firm." The woman playfully slapped

Derrick on the arm before extending her hand toward Sarah. "I'm Maggie, Derrick's wife."

Sarah shook her hand, happy to find Jake's family so friendly.

"Now, let's get you both fed." Maggie took Sarah by the arm, leading her toward the table loaded with food. Jake and Derrick followed a short distance behind. Sarah realized from their heated voices that they were arguing about something Derrick had said, but she couldn't hear their discussion over the noise of the party and Maggie's friendly chatter.

"Don't mind Derrick. You know older brothers love to give younger brothers a hard time," Maggie said. "Jake told us all about you."

"He did?"

"Yes, last night at dinner he spoke very highly of you. But don't tell Jake I said anything. He's afraid we'll go home and tell his parents about you, and his mother will be on the next plane hoping to finally see her youngest son married."

"It's not like that. Jake and I are just friends," Sarah insisted, all this family focus on her relationship with Jake making her nervous.

Maggie offered her a knowing wink. "I know, but for the moment we'll just pretend. That way I can go home and talk you up during Sunday dinner. It'll help Jake get through Christmas without the usual round of nagging." Maggie giggled. Far from being insulted, Sarah found Maggie's happy mood infectious and instantly liked the woman.

Very quickly Jake and Sarah found themselves in the midst of the party, making and receiving introductions and enjoying the catered ribs, corn bread, and coleslaw. Despite the barbecue's LA flair, most of the guests were East Coast transplants easily spotted by their choice of clothing. The men wore chinos and polo shirts, while the women wore similarly styled chinos and blouses. Sarah breathed a sigh of relief, knowing her outfit fit in perfectly with the others. A few polo players mingled with the guests, their high boots, tight pants, and bright shirts a stark contrast to the muted tones of the crowd.

Sarah saw little of Jake after they hit the buffet table. He maintained his distance, never standing alone with her, always hovering on the other side of conversation circles, until at one point he stopped joining the discussions altogether. Instead, he chatted with his sister-in-law or played with his niece.

Sarah stood with a small group of guests, trying to pay attention to the conversation. Out of the corner of her eye, she watched Jake play with Megan, using his powerful biceps to lift her up and swing her around. In a way she was glad he kept his distance. It made their relationship clear. However, she wanted nothing more than to join him and hear him laugh with Megan.

"Why are you wasting your time at a union?" Brandon asked, pulling her attention back to the circle of people around her. She'd been standing with this group for some time discussing the film business. The whole time, Brandon, a young producer at Raven Pictures with an overdeveloped sense of his own importance, had gone out of his way to catch her attention.

"Someone has to protect the workers from management."

"Entertainment unions are a thing of the past. They'll all

be gone within the next five years. You should get out while you can. Raven has an opening." Brandon leaned in close, offering her a wink. "You're too pretty to work at MAG."

Sarah took a discreet step back, careful to keep smiling and remain friendly despite being annoyed. After all, she was here to make contacts, and judging by Brandon's anti-labor attitude, it was probably just a matter of time before a claim against Raven Pictures hit her desk. "Thanks, but I'm happy at MAG."

"Suit yourself." Brandon shrugged.

"So, Brandon, what do you think about the Cornerstone Pictures deal?" another producer asked, taking his attention away from Sarah. She breathed a sigh of relief. Though on one level Brandon's attention was flattering, his personality couldn't match Jake's.

Sarah turned to watch Jake chase Megan around a table before sending her off to play with the other children. She thought about joining him but changed her mind when she saw Derrick approach him. His brother and sister-in-law already had suspicions. She wasn't about to confirm them. Giving Brandon her full attention, she hoped to make it clear to everyone, especially Jake's family, that they weren't a couple. If only she could make it clear to herself.

Jake watched Sarah, noticing the way she hung on Brandon's every word. Jake knew the man; he had a reputation in the industry as a sleazeball incapable of drafting a coherent contract. What was Sarah doing, spending so much time talking to him? She was too smart to have an interest in a guy like him. If she did develop an interest in Brandon, he had no one to blame but himself. Hadn't he spent the whole afternoon avoiding her, even though he wanted nothing more than to spend time with her?

"Better not let this one get away," Derrick said, slapping him on the back and handing him a bottle of beer. "I watched her out-debate Ron on whether or not to codify a basic agreement. No easy feat, given his contract-negotiation experience."

"I'm glad you approve, but we're just friends," Jake growled, fighting back his rising jealousy as Brandon took Sarah's hand, pretending to read her palm.

Derrick shot him a disbelieving look. "Is that why you can't take your eyes off her?"

Jake took a deep drag off the beer bottle, cursing himself for having been so obvious. "It's complicated right now."

"So she's on the other side of the table. It's not like you're both working the opposite sides of the same case." Derrick laughed, but his humor quickly faded under the narrow-eyed look Jake shot him. "You aren't, are you?"

Jake focused his attention on the polo match, refusing to meet his brother's interrogating look. "We're not dating. We're just friends."

"I can't believe you'd do something like this."

"I'm telling you, Derrick, nothing has happened," Jake said through clenched teeth, offering a wave to an older woman he knew from another studio as she walked by.

"Does anyone at Lion know?"

"Just Steve."

"Can you trust him?"

"Of course. He's my best friend."

"Good. Because if Lion Studios finds out—"

"Hey, drop the big-brother routine," Jake snapped, struggling to control the volume of his voice. The last thing he wanted to do was cause a scene.

"Then don't give me the swinging-bachelor routine," Derrick hissed, his face stern in a way strangely reminiscent of their father, a look Jake detested.

"Don't give me one of Dad's lectures."

"You know what he'd say if he heard this. You could be fired, disbarred. The arbitrator could sanction you, and Lion Studios could sue you both for everything you own. You'd be ruined, professionally and financially."

"It's none of your business."

"Someone needs to knock some sense into that thick head of yours."

Jake didn't answer. Hearing Derrick lay out the consequences suddenly made them all too real. He'd come to LA to prove to his family he could succeed without their help. Now, here he was, threatening to ruin it all for what seemed to Derrick like a simple fling. Jake tossed back the last of the beer, slamming the thick glass bottle down onto the table. "I don't need you telling me what to do."

Derrick leaned back a little, surprised by the outburst but definitely not cowed.

"Then think of her, Jake." Derrick stepped closer, his voice barely above a whisper. "Do you really want to ruin her career?"

Derrick walked off, joining Maggie, who watched them with a worried look. Derrick took Maggie's hand, then whispered into her ear, obviously explaining the situation. Her worried look quickly changed into one of surprise followed by nervous concern.

Jake looked at Sarah, jealousy flaring inside him when

Brandon pulled her close to give a passing waiter room. Jake resisted the urge to storm across the grass, push Brandon aside, throw his arm around Sarah's shoulders, and plant a large kiss on her tantalizing lips. He glanced at Derrick, noticing the way his brother and sister-in-law watched him. They looked as if they'd throw themselves on top of him if he made any move toward Sarah. It was typical Derrick dramatics, since Jake hadn't made a move for Sarah all afternoon.

Jake pushed down his rising anger as he watched Brandon and Sarah chat. She seemed to sense him watching, because she turned, offering him a sweet smile before resuming her conversation. Suddenly, Jake felt like a fool. He was torturing himself over a woman who probably wasn't interested in him. Hadn't she told him numerous times she didn't even want to be friends? But the look in her eyes when they'd almost kissed, the fiery way she'd glanced at him in her condo before the premiere, told him something different.

Plunging his hand into a nearby ice bucket, he grabbed another beer. He hated playing this game. He preferred to be direct, honest, to pursue his goals in a straightforward manner. Instead, he'd acted like a deceitful liar, intruding in Sarah's life and pushing his friendship on her even when she resisted because of her career. It would serve him right if Brandon stole her away.

As Jake watched her, Derrick's words rang in his ears. No matter what his feelings or how much he wanted her, he couldn't ruin her career. But he couldn't let her go. He didn't even know if she wanted him. Jake cursed under his breath for allowing himself to get into this crazy position. He'd look like a fool if this blew up in his face and took down his career with it. Though he hated to think about it, it was time to put an end to the situation.

The late-afternoon sun dipped behind a tall row of trees, casting shadows across the players and the grass. A cool breeze passed over the park, giving Sarah a little chill as she stood near the fence watching the end of the last polo match. The riders impressed her with their ability to control the huge animals in the thick of play and still keep track of the ball and their teammates. Despite the thrilling game, her heart sank a little while she stood alone on the sidelines watching. She'd barely seen Jake since she spotted him talking to Derrick. In fact, the jovial, smiling Jake she'd arrived with had disappeared, replaced by a somber-looking man who had few smiles for anyone except Megan.

"Perhaps we should get going?" Jake suggested, coming up behind her.

She turned to him, the smile quickly fading from her lips at the sight of his stern face.

"In a moment. The game is almost over, and it's a tie." She turned back to the field, rubbing her arms to keep warm.

He leaned against the fence next to her, his elbow tantalizingly close to hers. "Who are you rooting for?"

"The red team. They managed to come back after a bad beginning."

The game continued for another five minutes, the red team playing with a strength and conviction the gold team could not match. Finally, one rider slammed the ball with his mallet, sending it into the goal and scoring the winning point. Sarah jumped up and down, cheering and clapping with the other onlookers and the remaining barbecue guests who now stood at the fence watching the game end.

"I never knew polo could be so much fun," Sarah said, hoping to draw Jake out of his sullen mood. "I thought only foreign princes and British royalty enjoyed the sport. Thanks for inviting me."

"My pleasure. Did you meet many people?"

"I met quite a few, including a writer for *Hidden Pleasures.* Dinah will be excited when I tell her."

"What did you think of Brandon?"

Was that jealousy Sarah detected in his voice? It couldn't be, but it did make her wonder. "He's nice but arrogant."

"Like me?"

"No, nothing like you."

He stared at her for a moment, his blue eyes studying her face, betraying no emotion. She struggled to keep her own emotions from showing. *Friendship.* They were friends. She couldn't read any more into it than that, no matter what her heart urged her to see in his expression.

"I'm glad to hear it." Jake smiled with some of his previous flirtatious mirth, though the smile failed to light up his eyes. He turned away, fixing his gaze on the riders maneuvering their mounts off the field. "We'd better get going."

"Sure." Sarah tried not to show her disappointment as she followed Jake back to his car. He was quiet as he held the door open for her and remained silent as he got in, started the engine, and guided the Porsche back down the hill toward Sunset Boulevard.

Jake silently cursed the sudden awkwardness between them. He knew his brother was right, but something in him rebelled against it. He'd thought of almost nothing but Sarah for the past two weeks, holding back, being careful when he wanted to rush in. He knew she felt the same way. He'd caught her looking at him many times throughout the barbecue, and yesterday, on the jogging path, when the urge to kiss her had almost gotten the better of him. All he wanted was to touch her, hold her, smother her lips with his, taste her sweetness, and inhale her delicate scent.

Every time he shifted, he caught a glimpse of her hand resting tantalizingly on her knee. His palms itched with the urge to cover her small hand with his and feel the soft warmth of it under his grip.

In frustration, he slammed the car into gear, gripping the wheel with both hands and struggling to concentrate on the winding Palisades road. He'd wanted to spend the afternoon with her, yet he'd been forced to maintain his distance. That still hadn't been enough to distract Derrick. How many others had noticed? Or had they all only noticed the way Brandon monopolized Sarah's attention?

"Do you want to watch the sunset over the ocean?" he asked, unable to let the day or Sarah go just yet.

"Yeah, that sounds great."

Another awkward silence fell between them. Jake guided the car down toward Pacific Coast Highway, where the high mountains of the Palisades gave way to the Santa Monica cliffs overlooking the pier. Drumming his fingers on the steering wheel, he racked his brain for something to say, but nothing of substance came to mind. For the first time in years he was at a loss for words.

Turning into a small parking lot off the highway, he pulled the car into a spot with a perfect view of the beach and the sunset. The sun hung low over the water, glittering in the current and highlighting the surfers bobbing on the waves. Rollerbladers, joggers, and bicyclists hurried by on the paved walkway cutting through the center of the beach, fleetingly becoming silhouettes as they passed in front of the setting sun. The sound of the waves crashing against the sand reached them along with the screams of children playing near the water with their parents.

It was time to talk and put some distance between them before it was too late, but he couldn't speak. Out of the corner of his eye, he noticed the way Sarah shivered. "If you're cold, we can leave."

"No, I want to see the sunset."

"We can see it better from my place." Jake cursed the words the second they left his mouth. Here he was, trying to distance himself from her in an effort to protect both of their careers, and he was inviting her back to his place.

"Where do you live?" she asked in a curious voice, giving him enough hope to continue. Ignoring the way Derrick's warning echoed in his mind, he pointed up toward a modern glass building perched back above the cliff. She turned around in the seat to take it in, her eyes opening wide in amazement.

She let out a low whistle. "Lion Studios must pay well."

"Maybe I can get you a job there." It would make things a whole lot easier if she said yes.

"No thanks. It's tempting, but I'm not ready to sell my soul just yet." She laughed, rubbing her arms against the evening chill. It was all he could do to keep from wrapping his arms around her to keep her warm. "I suppose you want to show me your art collection?"

"If you want to see it. I also have a nice collection of wines and maybe some cheese and crackers," he offered with a wide smile, but it quickly faded. "Besides, I think we need to talk."

She raised one eyebrow. "You think your condo is the best place to do it?"

"It's warmer than here, closer than your place, and quieter than a restaurant." He struggled not to hold his breath while she remained silent, obviously pondering his suggestion. Everything about it was wrong, but he hoped she wouldn't turn him down. Her hesitation worried him, so he decided to sweeten the deal. "No strings attached."

She studied him for a moment with a look he couldn't read, then nodded. "All right."

He wanted to ball a fist in triumphant excitement, but instead he calmly pushed the starter button, snapping the Porsche's engine back to life. In less than five minutes they pulled into the covered driveway beneath the overhang of his condo complex.

"Very impressive," she said when a valet hurried forward to take Jake's car.

"This is nothing. Wait until you see the inside."

It wasn't a lie. Sarah's jaw dropped open in both surprise and awe when she followed him into the condo. The sizable living room was decorated in sleek modern furniture with a black leather sofa and matching ottoman. The condo faced the ocean, with an entire wall of floor-to-ceiling windows offering a magnificent view of the sunset. Outside the windows, a stone patio ran the length of the condo, accessible through a sliding-glass door.

"Go on outside. I'll get the wine." He walked toward the kitchen while she stepped outside, taking in the sight of the ocean stretching out toward the horizon.

To live like this, she thought, leaning on the stone railing and inhaling the salty evening air. It was a far cry from her view of the street, and for a moment she pictured herself living here, waking up every morning to the sight of waves breaking on the beach, enjoying breakfast with Jake while the gulls swung down over the water. Catching herself, she shook the images from her head. She wasn't ready to throw away her career or cheat actors out of their hard-earned money in order to get a life like this.

Then what are you doing here? she thought, wandering the length of the patio. She should have turned down his offer, asked him to take her home, but instead she'd agreed. He wanted to talk, and she wanted to hear what he had to say. He was probably planning to clarify their relationship, to give her the big speech about being nothing more than friends. She wasn't looking forward to hearing it, but she needed the cold dose of reality to stop her emotions from running away with her.

Another sliding-glass door leading to what she assumed was the master bedroom stood at the far end of the patio. Cupping her hands on the glass to block out the light, she peeked in, trying to get a good look at the heart of this bachelor pad. A king-sized bed sat against the far wall, covered in a deep brown microfiber comforter.

A slight cough caught her attention. She snapped up straight, embarrassed to have him catch her being so nosy.

"Impressive, isn't it?" he asked, placing two wineglasses and a bottle of wine on the small iron patio table. The soft strains of a jazz quartet drifted down from the outdoor speakers installed under the eaves.

"Pardon?" His bedroom was nice, but it wasn't *that* impressive.

He filled one of the glasses. "The view. Isn't it great?"

"Oh, yes, definitely," Sarah stammered, beating a quick retreat from the bedroom door to the table and taking the glass of wine he held out to her.

"What did you think I meant?"

"The view, of course." Sarah sat down, struggling to rein in her wandering mind. *Friends,* she reminded herself, taking a deep sip of wine. They were only friends.

Jake dragged the other metal chair next to hers, positioning it so they could both watch the sun descend toward the sparkling water. She wished he'd sat across the table from her, but she couldn't be rude and move. Instead she concentrated on the ocean, watching a family on the beach pack up their umbrella and blankets. The passing cars on the street below drowned out the sound of the waves, but she caught it from time to time on the breeze when the lights at either end of the road turned red, temporarily halting traffic.

"How long have you lived here?" she asked, drumming her fingers on the table in time to a spicy jazz number.

"Almost three years. I bought it before the market went crazy."

"Good investment."

She finished her wine, and he reached behind her for the bottle. She caught the scent of his aloe shaving cream. It hit her senses with as much force as the wine.

"You want some more?" he asked, holding up the bottle.

She thought about refusing, but with the sun almost below

the horizon and the lights of the Ferris wheel on the pier beginning to shine, she wasn't ready to leave yet.

"Sure." She held out her glass, and instead of taking it from her, he placed his hand over hers to keep the glass steady as he poured.

While he poured, she studied his face in the soft evening light. Despite all the problems between them, here was a man who knew how to make a woman feel special, who was too sure of his own success to ever be threatened by hers. He knew what he wanted and wasn't afraid to go after it, no matter what the consequences. And there were consequences, though none seemed to come to mind at the moment.

Instead her senses hummed at the feel of his warm skin on hers, the strength of his fingers curled around her hand. The closeness simultaneously disturbed and thrilled her. It was wrong, and she knew it, but she still couldn't bring herself to ask him to take her home.

He twisted the bottle to prevent it from dripping, and their eyes met. Her breath caught in her throat as he held her gaze before letting go of her hand to pick up his glass. She watched him, working hard to control her breathing and the way her heart constricted with the knowledge that she couldn't have him.

They were silent for quite some time. Jake refilled his glass, keeping his attention fixed firmly on pouring. The last thing he wanted to do was spill wine all over her. Reaching behind her to put the bottle back in the ice bucket, he caught the lavender scent of her hair. He closed his eyes for a moment and breathed in the fresh smell. He shouldn't have brought her here. He should have taken her home or discussed the issue in the car. It was dangerous being this close. He sat back in his chair, racking his brain for some way to broach the subject of their friendship and the danger of tempting fate. For the first time in his life, he couldn't make one argument in favor of a solid case.

"You know we can't really be friends." He forced the words out, regretting every one of them.

Sarah fingered the stem of her glass, gently biting her bottom lip. In the distance, a gull screeched as it dipped down toward the beach.

"Why?" she asked, her eyes fixed on the ocean. The sun had slipped below the horizon, but the thin clouds hanging overhead still burned with delicate shades of orange and pink. The lights of the Santa Monica pier grew brighter as the sky grew darker, reflecting off the ocean just beyond the breakers.

"Because, as my brother was so kind to remind me, I'm not usually friends with women."

She placed her wineglass on the table, then turned to him. The fading sunlight gave her face a soft glow, illuminating the blond highlights in her hair. It was all he could do to not touch her cheek or cover her lips with his. "I gathered that."

"I'm also not the kind of guy to ruin a woman's professional reputation."

Sarah glanced over his shoulder, concentrating on some spot in the distance. It broke his heart to see obvious pain fade her beautiful smile. He hated himself for being the cause of it.

A lively jazz tune filled the silence between them. Sarah let out a deep sigh, looking back toward the speakers hanging under the eaves of the balcony above his.

"I've always liked this song," she said wistfully.

Jake stood, taking her hand and pulling her up out of the chair. "Me too. It's one of my favorites, so let's not ruin it."

He swung her around, catching her in a loose embrace before sweeping them along the length of the balcony in an impromptu waltz. She followed his steps, the light coming back into her face. The music increased slightly in tempo, and Jake swung her out, then twirled her back in.

"You're pretty good." Sarah laughed, following his fluid box step around the width of the balcony.

"I took lessons in college." He twirled her out, then pulled her back, the force of the move sending her bumping into his chest. Wrapping his arms around her waist, he held her close before dropping her into an exaggerated dip. She giggled, playing along with his clumsy dance.

"I bet you didn't know I was so light on my feet." He smiled, pulling her up and spinning her in place.

"I never would have guessed it," she said, laughing, the sound charming his senses. It felt good to make her happy, and for the first time in months all the boredom and frustration of living in LA left him. He felt a sense of peace, one he wasn't about to lose.

Pulling her close again, he swayed gently to the slowed tempo of the music. Sarah slipped her hands over his shoulders, her bright eyes meeting his. He studied them, seeing in their depths a sense of hope and something else he couldn't name but knew he'd been missing for a long time.

"You're beautiful," he whispered, covering her lips with

his before she could object. Wrapping her arms around his neck, she met his kiss with equal passion. He pulled her closer, the subtle warmth of her embrace filling his senses. For one moment he forgot about everything except the gentle weight of her arms on his shoulders and the true emotion in her lips.

A car honked on the street below, breaking the spell. Sarah stepped back, the sincerity in her eyes catching Jake by surprise. Pushing aside her hair, he traced the line of her jaw. The warm feelings he'd enjoyed only a moment before slowly faded as he watched the worry steadily creep into her eyes.

"Jake," she began, but he laid a finger on her lips.

"Shh. It'll all work out." He pulled her into a deep hug, kissing the top of her head before staring up at the first few stars of night. They'd just crossed numerous lines, but he didn't care, and he didn't want to go back. The challenge would be figuring out how to move forward. He'd never had a goal he hadn't reached, a prize he hadn't obtained, and being with Sarah would be no different. She wanted him as much as he wanted her. He felt it in the way she clung to him, her cheek resting against his chest. But the situation was still complicated. He could hardly ask her to quit MAG, and he wasn't about to quit Lion. Secrecy was the key to making this work. They'd have to keep a secret, a big one, until the arbitration was over. In his gut he knew it was wrong, but for the moment there was no other way. He wasn't about to lose her now. When it was all over, they'd both have their careers and each other, and it would all be worth it.

Sarah hugged Jake tightly, struggling against the competing desire to pull him closer and to push him away. She didn't know what to think or feel. One moment he was talking about the hopelessness of their situation, the next he'd pulled her into a kiss like none she'd ever experienced before. She'd felt something deep and meaningful in his lips, an honesty of feeling he didn't even try to hide. It called to her very core, sending shivers of excitement and fear racing through her body.

"Are you cold? We can go inside if you want." Jake stepped back, looking down at her. The tenderness in his eyes made her nearly throw herself back into his arms and demand he kiss away the torrent of emotions flooding her mind. Instead she wrapped her arms across her chest, noting the cool ocean breeze drifting over the balcony and glad for the excuse to keep from kissing him again.

"Yes, it is a little cold," she replied, stepping aside so he could open the sliding door.

"After you." He motioned her ahead, and she walked inside, taking in the semidarkness of the condo and the way the orange glow of the streetlights glinted off the modern steel furniture.

"Excuse me for a moment," Jake apologized, then turned and walked off down the hall.

She heard the bathroom door close, and all the love and peace she'd felt on the balcony disappeared as the horror of what they'd done quickly overcame her. In one moment she'd broken at least ten ethical rules, putting her whole career in jeopardy. What had seemed like a great idea while sitting outside in the ocean air suddenly seemed like a really bad nightmare. It wasn't like her to break rules. Five years ago she'd agonized over tearing off her mattress tag, but tonight she hadn't thought twice about kissing opposing counsel. What had come over her? Even if she wanted to blame it on the wine, she couldn't. This was her fault.

Looking around the dim condo, she spotted her purse near the door where she'd dropped it after taking leave of her senses in a wine-and-sunset-fueled stupor. Digging through the small bag, she quickly located her cell phone and called Dinah.

"Hey, what's up?" Dinah asked, caller ID obviously having identified Sarah before Sarah could identify herself.

"I need you to come pick me up," Sarah whispered, listening for Jake while cupping a hand over her mouth and the phone so he wouldn't hear her.

"Pick you up from where?"

"Santa Monica."

"I thought you were in the Palisades. Are you at Jake's?"

"Never mind. I'll explain everything when you get here." She quickly gave Dinah instructions on where to pick her up. "I'll meet you outside."

She hung up, then looked around the condo for a notepad. She found one next to the answering machine and quickly scribbled a note. Leaving it on the coffee table, she hurried to the door. Grabbing the doorknob, she stopped, a sense of guilt gripping her. She should at least wait and explain herself to Jake, but she didn't trust herself to be strong where he was concerned. If she had to face him or look into his caring eyes again, she knew everything would be lost, and she might as well quit MAG and move back to Richmond.

Once in the hallway, she practically ran to the elevator. She had to get out before Jake found the note and followed her. Jamming the call button, she breathed a sigh of relief when the doors instantly opened. Stepping inside, she punched the button for the lobby, then held down the close-door button. When the doors slid closed, she leaned back against the elevator wall, struggling to take deep breaths.

Why had she kissed him? Why? Because she had feelings for him, and something in her wanted to enjoy the freedom and excitement of her new life. After all, she was a modern woman with a career and needs. Why not enjoy the big city and have some fun?

Because it's wrong! her mind screamed.

The elevator doors opened, and she stepped out into the brightly lit lobby. Shame filled her, especially when the night doorman nodded his greeting.

"Shall I call a taxi, ma'am?" he asked.

She shook her head. "No, a friend is coming to pick me up."

He nodded a little too knowingly for Sarah's taste. Obviously, she wasn't the first woman to run out this front door in a hurry. She slipped outside, the cold night air offering a welcome sting. Hurrying off down the block, she shook her head in continued disbelief. Who was she kidding? She was no chick-lit heroine with a closetful of shoes and the morals of a tree sloth. No, she was Sarah Steele, MAG attorney with about five pairs of shoes, not including her jogging sneakers, and a very well-defined sense of right and wrong. What she had just done was wrong, very, very wrong. Or was it? She'd thrown caution to the wind and probably with it her career, and for what?

Sarah walked faster toward the corner, hoping to make it around the block before Jake came after her. Her mind kept going over the loving way he'd looked at her when he'd tilted her chin up, his eyes meeting hers. She'd seen something more in their blue depths than a manipulating lawyer looking to win a case. They'd held a certain tenderness and longing she felt deep in her heart.

No. She stopped herself, pausing at the corner and jamming the crosswalk button. She didn't feel anything for Jake except regret, and Jake didn't feel anything for her. He was just a better manipulator than she'd realized, and she'd been dumb enough to fall for his act.

The crosswalk light changed, and Sarah hurried across the street toward the hustle of Third Street Promenade. Standing outside the Coffee Pot coffeehouse, where she'd told Dinah to pick her up, she shook her head in continued disbelief at her own weakness. Wouldn't David just laugh if he could see her now? No, he couldn't know. No one except Dinah, Jake, and the doorman could ever know. If fate had any pity on her, she'd get through the next week and the arbitration without anyone finding out. All she had to do was avoid Jake and win the arbitration. A difficult but not impossible feat. She'd faced bigger obstacles before. As Dinah's car appeared down the road, Sarah waved to catch her attention, wondering if fate would smile so widely on her this time.

Chapter Nine

Sarah sat at her desk, finishing her third cup of coffee and feeling very old. In law school she could stay up all night with David at a party or perhaps his place and still make it through class, work, and an evening study session. However, David was no Jake, and she'd spent the whole night staring at the ceiling trying to get Jake out of her mind. She sighed at the memory of his lips on hers and the connection she'd felt in the warm tenderness of his touch.

No. She stopped herself, remorse settling in with the caffeine jitters. Suddenly her phone intercom buzzed, making her jump. She fumbled to put on her headset, then hit the button.

"Yes?'

"Come to my office, please, and bring the *Tidal Wave* file," Bonnie said before the line went dead.

Worry quickly replaced both the jitters and remorse as Sarah gathered up the file and headed down the hall. Thankfully, there wasn't any lingering physical evidence of her

evening indiscretion, just the overwhelming fear that someone would find out.

Sarah stopped dead outside Bonnie's office. Had Bonnie
found out? Maybe someone who worked at MAG lived in
Jake's building and saw her leaving last night?

The moment the worry popped into her head, Sarah
shook it away with a suppressed laugh. It was pretty unlikely
anyone on MAG's payroll could afford a place in Jake's
building. However, as she walked into Bonnie's office, the
worry instantly returned. There was one person at MAG
who could afford to live in Jake's building, and she was sitting right in front of Sarah.

"Sarah, this is Eva Jones, president of MAG," Bonnie introduced.

Eva held out her hand, forcing Sarah to overcome her
nervous stupor as they shook. Despite her general igno-
rance of movie and TV trivia, Sarah knew Eva Jones. She
was one of the lead actresses on *Hidden Pleasures* and a
veteran film and TV star with a reel extending back to the
1960s. Eva was stunning, with elegantly coiffed blond hair,
flawless makeup, and a very classy sense of style. Sarah
wasn't easily starstruck, but as she took a seat next to this
star, she felt a little giddy and guilty.

"Nice to meet you, Ms. Jones. I hope you didn't hit too
much traffic driving here from Santa Monica," Sarah remarked, thankful for the way LA traffic always provided a
ready subject for small talk. It gave her an easy way to find
out where Eva lived.

"I live in Beverly Hills, not Santa Monica," Eva snapped
with unnecessary indignation, reminding Sarah of exactly

why she was rarely starstruck. Meeting stars in person was usually a huge disappointment. However, the fact that Eva couldn't have seen her sneaking out of Jake's building gave her a small measure of comfort.

"Eva is here because Lion Studios refuses to pay basic cable residuals on the first season of *Hidden Pleasures*," Bonnie quickly intervened. "It looks like they're extending their practice beyond *Tidal Wave*."

"Lion Studios sold the first season to cable. Now they tell me they don't have to pay the full residuals rate stated in the Basic Agreement. They did that to me, one of their stars. Can you imagine what they're doing to lesser-known actors?" Eva huffed.

Bonnie turned to Sarah. "I was telling Ms. Jones how Lion Studios isn't paying any actors the correct basic cable residuals rate and that the *Tidal Wave* arbitration should settle the matter. If we win."

"We'd better win," Eva stated. "Especially since the whole town now knows about the arbitration."

She flung a copy of *The Hollywood Reporter* onto Bonnie's desk, folded back to reveal an article about the arbitration.

"I saw the article this morning," Bonnie responded, nodding for Sarah to take the trade magazine.

Sarah slowly lifted it off the desk and skimmed the article. Though it didn't mention either Sarah or Jake, it explained the arbitration issue in detail and the consequences if MAG lost.

"How'd they find out?" Sarah asked.

"Someone at Lion must have leaked the story," Bonnie

replied, offering Eva a nervous smile. It was the first time Sarah had seen Bonnie less than confident.

"MAG and the producers are set to renegotiate the Basic Agreement in June. If we lose the arbitration, not only do actors lose residuals, but MAG loses a pretty strong negotiating position. Every studio is watching to see how this arbitration goes," Eva stated, sitting back in her chair like a queen. "We have to win."

"We will," Bonnie concurred. "Sarah has a lot of experience fighting large corporations over interpretations of basic agreements. We practically hired her for this arbitration."

Sarah struggled to offer a confident smile even though she felt like a fraud. However, now was not the time to unload her guilty conscience. "Yes, I do have experience."

"Good. I trust you'll do your best to make sure we win," Eva continued. "Actors depend on residuals to get through the lean times. Imagine the financial devastation to our members if the studios suddenly stopped paying residuals. We can't let the studios get away with it."

"No, we can't," Sarah agreed, struggling against her fatigue to stay focused, professional, and above all to hide all evidence of worry. If either Eva or Bonnie knew how at risk the arbitration currently stood because of Sarah's uncontrollable hormones, they'd both be in her office flinging her personal effects out into the street. "MAG has always maintained that the residuals language in the Basic Agreement is clear and clearly supported by past industry custom and practice. When movies or network TV shows are sold to basic cable, residuals are due on the contracted-for sale price."

"Great," Eva replied, visibly delighted by Sarah's response. "So tell me how you plan to win."

Sarah launched into a detailed explanation of her arbitration strategy. The whole time, the sinking feeling in the pit of her stomach increased. She was a lying, cheating fraud. These women expected her to lock horns with Lion Studios and fight for the rights of actors. Instead, she'd locked lips with their senior counsel, putting the whole arbitration at risk. Her professional reputation and years of hard work as an attorney, along with all the money she'd spent putting herself through law school, were in jeopardy. She might not have revealed any MAG secrets during the sunset waltz—in fact, work had never come up—but that wouldn't matter to the arbitrator or MAG. The only hope of redeeming herself for the worst lapse of judgment in her life was to win the arbitration. Assuming she made it to the arbitration with her career intact.

After what seemed like hours, though in reality it was less than fifteen minutes, Eva stood, bringing an end to the informal meeting.

"Thank you for all your hard work," Eva said, shaking their hands. "I have an early call time, so I need to go."

Eva departed, leaving Sarah alone with Bonnie, who flipped through a stack of letters to be signed.

Sarah slowly gathered up her file, hesitating, wondering just how much, if anything, she should say. If she confessed, she'd be fired. If she kept silent, then the truth might come out at the arbitration. Sarah wasn't sure which was worse. "Are you sure you still want me on this arbitration?"

Bonnie continued reading her letters, signing one before picking up the next. "I wasn't lying when I told Eva I practically hired you for this arbitration."

"But I wonder if my knowing Jake Rappaport wouldn't create a conflict of interest." It wasn't quite the truth, but it was as close as Sarah was willing to come. After all, so far it was only one passionate kiss. Hardly a relationship.

Bonnie glanced up with a scrutinizing look, making Sarah regret opening her big mouth about Jake. It seemed the number of things she regretted about Jake were beginning to pile up.

"You said he was just a former classmate."

"He is, was. We're just acquaintances—we don't really speak much outside work. We don't speak at all, in fact." Sarah waited for a lightning bolt to strike her dead and put her out of her misery, but it didn't come. "I just know how important this arbitration is to MAG. If Lion leaked the story, then they know they have a weak case, and they're looking for support or some kind of strategy. I don't want anything, no matter how small and insignificant, to be used against us or ruin our chances of winning."

"I agree. I think the article does show their weakness, but I wouldn't worry about Lion trying to exploit any kind of past relationship between you and Jake, especially one so insignificant." Bonnie tossed down her pen, leaning back in her chair. "Half the people in this department went to school with or know someone on the other side of the table. Besides, I've worked with Jake Rappaport long enough to know he won't let any personal feelings get in the way of trying to win. It's up to you to do the same. You can do that, can't you?"

"Definitely," Sarah replied with fake confidence. She could arbitrate this claim without allowing her personal life to affect it. But would he? Hadn't he already said that a good lawyer knows how to look for advantages, no matter how small, in order to win? Well, she'd just handed him the biggest advantage imaginable. Only she wasn't the sole guilty party. If he used the advantage, he'd take himself down with her. They'd both face disciplinary action, making it unlikely he'd say anything to anyone, much less the arbitrator, about their personal relationship. All Sarah had to do was dedicate every waking moment of the next few days to fine-tuning her argument. She had to win. She had no choice.

"Good." The phone rang, and Bonnie checked the caller ID. "If you'll excuse me, I have to take this call."

Sarah nodded, then fled the office. What had she done? What had she gotten herself into? Nothing, absolutely nothing. It was a one-time mistake, and it would never happen again.

"Jake Rappaport is on your line," the secretary said as Sarah passed her desk. Sarah stopped dead, thankful her back was to the secretary so she couldn't see the look of panic decorating her face. Sarah's heart began to race, and it took all the control she could muster not to break into a cold sweat as she turned to face her.

"Tell him I'm busy and I'll call him back."

"He's called three times," she offered apologetically, but Sarah knew there was nothing the secretary could say to make her take this call.

"Tell him I'll call him back," Sarah repeated in a more authoritarian, bosslike tone, feeling a little guilty as the secretary looked down at the phone, visibly cringing. Slowly, the secretary picked up the line, giving Jake the message in a rushed voice, then quickly scribbling down his reply.

"Did he start yelling?" Rachel asked from the doorway of her office.

"What?" Sarah asked, caught off guard by Rachel's question.

"Rappaport. Did he finally start yelling at you? Usually you take his calls. You're the only one who does."

"Oh, yeah," Sarah breathed, somewhat relieved. "Yup, he's a screamer, and I don't put up with screamers."

"He wants you to call him back," the secretary interrupted, handing Sarah the pink message note. "He says it's important."

Sarah walked into her office, struggling to steady her breathing as she fell into her chair. Her cell phone suddenly vibrated into life, bouncing around on the desk. Snatching it up, she checked the screen, confirming her fears. Jake. She wasn't about to answer it. In fact, she stared at it, afraid to touch even one button for fear it might accidentally answer. Instead she waited as it continued to vibrate in her hand before rolling to voice mail. This was the third time she'd ignored his call.

He didn't leave frantic messages like David had when she'd dumped him. Instead, Jake's messages were cool, measured, controlled. She had to admire him even if she never wanted to see him again. She flipped open the phone, but this time he hadn't left a message. It didn't matter. His messages never offered more than the basics, no matter how much she tried to read into his name and phone number. As Sarah slipped the phone into her purse, she sighed, faintly depressed by the whole ordeal. What she wouldn't give to have an uncomplicated relationship with a man.

Jake tossed his headset onto the desk, resisting the urge to throw the golf ball in his hand against the wall. The divot would be difficult to explain to his boss, and the last thing he wanted was anyone questioning his personal life. What was he doing, still calling Sarah after two days of receiving nothing but voice mail? He wasn't some lovesick college boy, so why was he making a fool out of himself? Because he didn't like failure, and her silence felt like failure.

It was failure. He thought he'd sealed the deal Sunday night. Then he'd stepped into his living room to find nothing but an apology note and an empty condo. For the first time he understood what all his previous dates must have felt when he'd used some weak excuse to dump them on their doorstep after a lackluster outing. It made him realize what a jerk he'd been.

A knock on the office door pulled him out of his thoughts.

"Come in," he barked.

"Not enough coffee this morning?" Steve asked, strolling in with a copy of *The Hollywood Reporter* under his arm and closing the door behind him.

"You could say that," Jake mumbled, running the golf ball between his hands.

"Word on the street is that you've been screaming more than usual this week." Steve pulled out one of the steel and leather chairs positioned in front of Jake's desk and sat down. "What's wrong?"

How much did he want Steve to know? "Labor relations problems."

Steve raised a curious eyebrow at Jake. "You mean the MAG attorney? Wow. What did she do to get so far under your skin?"

Jake slapped his hand on the desk, making the pens and pencils jump. "No one's 'under my skin.' "

"So I see," Steve replied, lounging back in the chair. "What's going on?"

Jake sat back, attempting to regain self-control. Anger wasn't the way to solve his problem. He needed to think clearly, logically, instead of like some emotional wreck. "Things are a little complicated right now."

Steve cocked a suggestive eyebrow. "Are you two dating?"

"No. But we crossed a few lines." Jake looked out the window at the soundstages covering the lot. This was one time he didn't feel like bragging about a conquest.

Steve let out a low whistle. "Wow, you must have it bad."

"Have what?" Jake snapped, in no mood for Steve's humor.

"A real thing for a woman."

Jake gripped the golf ball hard in his hand, wishing he could crush it. Hearing Steve state the truth so bluntly made him feel weak, vulnerable. He couldn't afford to look weak, not on the eve of a major arbitration with a bunch of junior lawyers craving his job. Still, Jake had to admit that Steve was right. He had it bad for Sarah, so bad he'd allowed it to interfere with his better judgment and quite possibly his career. And for what? One kiss and a good-bye note? What had seemed like a good idea a few weeks ago was suddenly blowing up in his face and threatening to take down his career.

"Judging from your happy demeanor, she obviously isn't into you," Steve hazarded.

Jake steepled his fingers under his chin, studying his friend. He'd always been in charge of relationships, calling the shots or putting an end to it when things got too serious.

Now Sarah called the shots, and for the first time he felt the uncertainty of not knowing where he stood. "I don't know. She didn't stick around long enough to tell me."

"This is bad." Steve leaned forward, tossing *The Hollywood Reporter* onto Jake's desk, faceup and open to another article about the arbitration. "Did you see this?"

"I saw it," Jake grumbled, not bothering to pick it up.

"How'd they find out?"

"Larry Allen has been planting stories without consulting me. He wants to ratchet up the pressure on MAG before the negotiations start."

"Well, let's hope the pressure doesn't make your girlfriend snap."

"She's not my girlfriend," Jake grumbled, quickly clicking the end of his ballpoint pen.

"My point exactly." Steve leaned forward, tapping the article with one finger. "You can't leave her hanging, saying who knows what to whom. Could end your career."

"She can't say anything without ruining her own career."

"Who says she won't, just to get back at you? Women are funny like that."

Jake hated to think of the situation in such selfish, self-preserving terms, but Steve was right. "She won't return my calls."

"Then you'd better find a way to speak with her. Complain to her boss or something."

"And say what?" Jake asked sarcastically. "Bonnie, can you have Sarah call me about our evening together? Oh, and if you don't mind not mentioning this to the arbitrator or the state bar, I'd really appreciate it."

"I don't know, but you've got to do something. All this screaming, and we'll lose every secretary in the building." Steve chuckled before his BlackBerry chirped and he looked at the screen. "Duty e-mails. I've got to run."

"What would you do?" Jake asked.

Steve shrugged, barely thinking about the question before he answered. "Offer her some emotion. Nothing wins a woman over faster than a little male emotion."

"How would you know?" Jake laughed, trying to imagine Steve expressing any emotion, genuine or fake, to a woman.

"I had it bad once," Steve admitted, shaking his head as he turned to leave. "Worst two weeks of my life."

He slipped out the door, pulling it closed behind him.

Jake walked to the window, leaning an arm against the cool glass, contemplating how to get Sarah to talk to him. He had to know where they stood, though his reason for wanting to know was more than professional. He'd thought about showing up at her place but didn't want to look like a stalker. Thinking about her and the very real possibility of losing her had kept him up for the last two nights. Steve was right. Jake had a thing for Sarah. He had it bad enough to allow her to affect him in a way no other woman had before. The question was, did she have a thing for him?

Across the street, a small crew installed a billboard advertising the *Hidden Pleasures* holiday special. Watching the workers lower the sign into place, an idea struck him. He hurried to his computer and pulled up the company directory. Searching through the names, he stopped when he found the one he was looking for. Dialing the phone, he wondered if he'd lost his mind. He was taking a huge risk, but there was one other person on the Lion lot who knew their secret, and, with luck, she could help him.

"Come on, enough moping. We're going out." Dinah flipped on the bedroom light, waking Sarah up from her after-work nap.

"I'm not moping," Sarah protested, burying her head under a pillow.

"Well, you're not exactly partying either." Dinah yanked the pillow off Sarah's head. "Come on, we're not spending another evening at home. Get up."

"I like being at home," Sarah snapped, pulling the blanket over her head.

"Yeah, well, tonight you're going out." Dinah threw open Sarah's closet and started tearing through the contents. "Where's the satin top with the spaghetti straps you bought when we went shopping? Oh, here it is. And which pair of jeans do you prefer, the dark wash or the light?"

Sarah reluctantly sat up, looking at the two pairs of jeans Dinah held up. There was no point protesting, especially not with Dinah looking so determined. "The dark ones. I tried to drown my sorrows in a pint of ice cream today."

"Ouch. Well, happy hour at El Amigo ought to cure that."

"El Amigo?" Sarah asked, catching the dark jeans Dinah tossed at her and quickly slipping them on.

"Everyone goes to El Amigo for happy hour. Trust me, you can't be depressed there."

An hour later, Sarah followed Dinah into the noisy El Amigo Mexican restaurant. Despite looking very put together for someone who'd spent the last two hours sleeping, Sarah didn't exactly feel ecstatic about being out in public. However, glancing around the bar, Sarah quickly realized Dinah was right. No one could mope at El Amigo.

A large, rectangular room filled with a vibrant mix of college students and young executives dominated the restaurant's first-floor lounge. A typical bar filled the back half of the room, with the crowd breaking into periodic fits of excited yelling as they watched their favorite college football teams duke it out on the big-screen TV. The front half of the room was just as crowded but more sedate as people lounged on the numerous couches enjoying margaritas and appetizers. The various *U*-shaped arrangements of the couches gave the area a cozy, living-room kind of feel. Beyond the front room and all along the expansive upstairs balcony, diners enjoyed Mexican food among the bright tile work and colorful hacienda decor.

"Quick, there's two seats." Dinah grabbed Sarah's arm, pulling her toward the two places being vacated on the sofa near the fireplace. As they sat down, Dinah smiled at the handsome man next to her, and he smiled back. Sarah sighed, not seeing much hope for conversation with Dinah tonight.

"I'll get the drinks," Sarah said, taking in the brisk business at the bar.

"Get two margaritas. They're famous and strong."

"Two margaritas it is." Sarah pushed herself up off the plush couch and made her way through the crowd toward the bar. She waited a moment before an opening cleared, then stepped forward.

"What'll you have?" the bartender asked, smiling at her with the TV-star good looks almost required of all LA bartenders. Sarah wondered why she couldn't have fallen for someone like him, someone who didn't come with the baggage of being opposing counsel. Leave it to her to make a fling so involved.

"Two margaritas," she ordered, forcing herself to stop dwelling on her mistakes or, more specifically, her most recent mistake.

"Coming right up." He winked. Placing two large cactus-stemmed glasses on the bar, he splashed in a little margarita mix followed by a heavy dose of tequila. Sarah almost told him to go light on the alcohol, then changed her mind. Maybe a little tequila would succeed where the ice cream had failed. Besides, a slight buzz might take the edge off being depressed in a crowd of happy, cheering people.

"That'll be eight bucks."

Sarah opened her purse, digging for her wallet, when someone handed a ten-dollar bill over her shoulder. "Keep the change," a familiar voice instructed.

Sarah turned to see Jake behind her. Dinah wasn't kidding when she said everyone came to El Amigo for happy hour.

"No, wait, I want to pay," Sarah called to the bartender, but he was already at the other end of the bar, chatting with two buxom women.

"Don't worry about it. Besides, it's my pleasure," Jake said. "In fact, let me buy you dinner."

"I've already eaten." She crossed her arms over her chest, trying to fight the way her body hummed when Jake stood so close. She regretted eating so much double fudge ice cream and skipping her morning jog, then wondered if her makeup hid the dark circles under her eyes. The last thing she wanted was to look like she'd been missing him or pining for him or anything about him. As usual he was impeccably dressed in a black sweater and tan pants, his hair swept back off his forehead.

"Then dessert." He offered her a playful smile she wanted to slap off his face for being almost too irresistible. Almost. She might dislike him, but she also wanted to kiss him.

"I can't abandon my friend." She pointed toward the couch where Dinah sat enjoying a lively conversation with the handsome man.

Jake chuckled, and Sarah tried to ignore the way the deep sound made her skin tingle. "It looks like your friend won't miss your company."

Sarah picked up the margaritas and headed back toward the couch, ignoring Jake despite being all too aware of him following her. As she approached the couch, Dinah's eyes met hers before flitting to Jake. She offered Sarah a weak smile, giving her the sneaking suspicion that Dinah knew something about this strange coincidence.

"Did you know he'd be here?" Sarah hissed into Dinah's ear as she sat down, handing her the other margarita.

Dinah sipped her drink, avoiding Sarah's eyes. "It might have been mentioned at work today. Besides, you two need to talk." Dinah quickly turned back to her new male friend, leaving Sarah to stew on the couch alone. She looked up at Jake, who stood over her.

"Can we go outside and talk?" he asked, ignoring the way Sarah glared at him, her foot tapping the tile floor in nervous anger.

"No."

To her horror, the pager in the hand of the man next to her lit up, and he and his date got up and left. Jake quickly sat down beside her, pushed up against her by the woman on his left who took the other vacated seat.

"We need to talk," Jake insisted.

"No, we don't." Sarah didn't look at him. Instead she looked straight ahead, trying to find a way out of this situation. Dinah had driven, so she couldn't leave. If Sarah went outside, he'd only follow her. She could go to the ladies' room, but the idea of spending the next two hours in there wasn't exactly appealing. If he wanted to talk, then they'd talk.

"I would have driven you home. There was no need to sneak out on me," Jake said in a low voice, leaning in close to be heard. The smell of her honeysuckle perfume filled his senses, and he resisted the urge to kiss her silky white neck.

"Yes, there was," she replied, leaning away from him. "You and I both know how bad a personal relationship, no matter how brief or miscalculated, is to our professional careers."

He took a sip of his margarita, knowing she was right but feeling something else, something that had been playing on his mind for months. "There's more to life than a career."

She twisted around on the couch to face him, her eyes wide. "I can't believe you, of all people, would say such a thing."

"I hardly believe it myself."

"Well, I don't believe it, especially not coming from someone who wants nothing more than success and money."

Jake started to doubt Steve's advice to discuss feelings and show some emotion but decided to keep trying. Since meeting Sarah, for the first time he wanted to be honest with her and himself. "At one time I did, but after seeing my brother and sister and how happy they are with their families, I feel as if something is missing."

"What's missing is the truth. I've seen you with starlets and your studio lawyer friend. You like women to fall at your feet, and you like to win, so much so that when a woman finally turns you down, you feel compelled to pursue her, especially if she's your opponent and might divulge a few secrets."

Jake felt as if he'd been slapped. He'd told her the truth, and she'd thrown it back in his face. "You're not entirely wrong, but you're far from right."

"Then why did you pursue me?"

Because I love you, Jake thought, the force of the emotion surprising him. He hadn't thought of her in those terms before. He'd never thought of any woman in those terms because he'd never met a woman like Sarah before. Despite the strength of his feelings, he couldn't say it aloud. Not in a crowded restaurant with her staring at him with such anger and disgust. He needed a plan, some way of dealing with the situation, of taking control and succeeding, but nothing came to mind. Anger welled inside him. Anger at Sarah and at himself for allowing her to make him feel like a fool.

"What about you? You play the innocent, but you didn't say no when I invited you to my place, and you didn't seem to mind my kiss. Maybe you thought you could please your new boss by getting a few secrets out of *me*?"

Her eyes opened wide, then narrowed in anger. "I would never stoop so low."

"Wouldn't you? After all, you're adept at exploiting small

technicalities to win cases. Very clever, Miss Steele. I think we both crave career success, only I'm a little more honest about it." He regretted the words the second they left his mouth, knowing he'd lost control and hating the way it made him act and feel.

Hot anger flashed in her eyes before dissolving into a nervous vulnerability. Her grip tightened on her glass, and the glimmer of tears appeared in the corners of her eyes. He wanted to reach over and brush them away, pull her close and smooth away her fears and worries. However, her voice stopped him short.

"Yes, I crave success because—" she said, a slight quaver evident in her voice before she stopped. Running her thumb along the side of her glass, she wiped away a small trail of condensation. "Because it's all I have right now."

She stood, practically spilling her drink in her rush from the couch to the ladies' room.

"What did you say to her?" Dinah asked, pinning Jake with accusing eyes before making her excuses to the man next to her and hurrying off to help Sarah.

Jake stormed out the entrance, marching past the valet to retrieve his car from the front row of the parking lot. Jumping inside, he gunned the engine and sped out onto Wilshire Boulevard. What the heck was he doing? He knew Sarah hadn't played him, so why had he said it? Because he wanted and needed the upper hand, and it had felt like the only way to get it.

Jamming the car into the next gear, he tore down the street toward the ocean and home. The way she'd looked at him tonight compared with the way she'd looked at him when they'd kissed grated on his mind. Unlike him, she wasn't a schemer. She'd never tried to take advantage of their friendship or to bag him because of his car or his paycheck. He'd been the one to make all the moves, to orchestrate everything. Then, when she'd been honest with him, instead of returning the favor, he'd thrown insults back in her face. He'd been a fool to think it would be so simple, that she would compromise herself more than she already had and think nothing of it. Wasn't it her integrity, her sense of right and wrong, standing up for the little guy, part of what he admired about her? Instead of admiring it, he'd asked her to sacrifice it for him, when in truth he should have been doing the sacrificing. But sacrificing for what? He'd made no promises. He hadn't even told her how he truly felt.

Turning in to his building, he parked the car and hurried toward the stairwell. He jogged up the stairs to his floor, but the exercise didn't cool his anger or clear his mind. Slamming the condo door closed, he flipped on the light, surprised by the overwhelming emptiness of the living room. At one time the expensive, ultramodern furniture had made him feel powerful and successful. Tonight, it felt cold and uninviting, especially with the prospect of another night alone staring him in the face. He stormed out onto the terrace, his hands gripping the stone railing. What was the point of a million-dollar view if there was no one to share it with?

Suddenly he knew what to do. He could have kicked himself for being so stupid and allowing his ego to get in the way of achieving his goal. He released his tight grip and flexed his fingers. What about his career? Hadn't the last year left him feeling bored and empty? Maybe his LA life made him seem shallow, but tonight, alone with no one to impress, he knew he wanted more than just the fast car and the corner office. There was only one woman he wanted to share a new life with, and he knew what he had to do to win her.

"Why did you do it?" Sarah asked, finally able to speak, her anger giving way to tired disappointment. She heard Dinah breathe a small sigh of relief as she guided the car down the road toward home.

"I thought you two needed to talk, and somewhere public was the best place to do it. Face it, Sarah, it took a lot of guts for him to call me and ask me to do it. He must care about you."

"No, he doesn't."

"Then why did he do it?"

"I don't know. Because he was losing, and he hates losing." Why *had* he done it? Jake didn't seem like the kind of man to run after a woman. "Besides, if he likes me, why was he so mean?"

"I heard you two talking. You weren't exactly pleasant."

"You're saying this is my fault?"

"No, but you didn't give him much of a chance to say anything. He's a man; he's not going to just come right out and say he loves you. Especially not when you're shooting daggers."

"He isn't about to say he loves me. He isn't about to say anything except he used me or accuse me of using him." Had she? Didn't she start all this with the hope he might reveal something in an unguarded moment? No, that had only been a brief thought, a weak excuse for why she should attend the premiere. How could it have backfired this badly?

"Come on, Sarah, there's more to this than the two of you trying to get information out of each other."

Sarah didn't answer, knowing Dinah was right but not wanting to believe it. Sunday she'd felt something she hadn't felt in years, and it had scared her so much, she'd scurried out of his place like a coward. Tonight, she should have listened to what he had to say, but she hadn't wanted the heartbreak of hearing another man tell her he didn't want her, because, despite everything, she loved Jake.

Leaning her head against the cool glass of the window, she fought back another round of tears. The idea of giving him up, of walking away from someone who respected her and went out of his way to make her feel special made her chest tighten. She cursed fate, wondering what she'd done to be so unlucky in love. If things had been different, they could have been together, and for the first time in a long time she could have had someone who truly cared about her. No, he didn't really care about her; or at least that's what she kept telling herself, trying to believe it was true. Loving Jake wasn't an option; it was a mistake, and she'd overcome it just like she'd overcome her feelings for David.

"Whatever is going on, I can't think about it right now. The arbitration is Friday, and if I don't win, I might as well pack up and go home. I can worry about Jake on Saturday."

Chapter Ten

Sarah sat in the conference room, nervously tapping her pen against the yellow legal pad in front of her. Her pantyhose itched, but she didn't dare scratch. There was already one run beneath her skirt, threatening to extend down her leg at any moment. The last thing she needed to do was make it worse. Not that today could get any worse. Once Jake sat down across the table and the arbitration began, everything would be set for a huge malpractice suit based on a very serious conflict of interest.

She should have made Bonnie remove her from the case, but that would have meant admitting everything, and how could she? Revealing her relationship with Jake would only get her fired, sending her packing back to Richmond. No, she'd keep silent and hope nothing ever came of it. After all, she hadn't told him anything about the case, never revealed any MAG secrets. She was guilty of nothing except being unable to control her natural urges.

Sarah looked down the length of the table to where the

arbitrator, Allan Elliot, sat pushing his wire-rimmed glasses up the bridge of his nose while Bonnie spoke to him. He wore a dark, ill-fitting suit with a slight sheen from too many pressings. Allan might be one of the most labor-friendly arbitrators around, but Sarah doubted his ability to sympathize with overwhelming natural urges.

Bonnie had been surprised when, during the arbitrator-selection process, they'd chosen Allan, and Lion Studios hadn't objected. Sarah was surprised too and wondered if Jake had had something to do with it. No, it was impossible. All he cared about was his career and collecting the accompanying accoutrements. He'd practically said so at El Amigo.

She hadn't heard from Jake since El Amigo. He hadn't called or e-mailed, and she'd been careful not to send anything to his office. His silence unnerved her, increasing her anxiety about today. Perhaps he was plotting revenge or some way to get back at her for challenging his ego. Even as she thought it, she didn't believe it. Whatever else she'd accused him of being, she knew he wasn't capable of ruining her simply because she'd refused him. If there was one thing she could count on, it was his ability to be and act like a professional. Besides, Jake had as much to lose by revealing their secret as she did, though the thought was less than comforting.

The ticking clock filled the room along with a secretary's high-pitched laugh from outside the door. The Lion Studios attorneys had yet to arrive. There'd been a bad accident on the freeway, and traffic all over town was practically at a standstill. Unfortunately, Sarah had left home before the accident and had no trouble getting to work. Leave it to fate to help her get to work on time. She wouldn't have minded a good excuse to be late or to postpone the arbitration.

The phone rang and Sarah jumped, not realizing just how tightly wound the silence and the stress had made her. Bonnie reached across the table, snatching the phone from its receiver. "Yes? Great. Thanks."

"They're here," Bonnie said to Sarah and Allan before dialing another number. "Karen, the Lion Studios people are here. Please escort them upstairs."

Bonnie took her place at the table, nodding assuredly to Sarah, who responded with the most confident nod she could muster. Sarah stopped tapping her pen and tried to relax. There was no turning back now. Whatever was going to happen was going to happen. She had no choice but to face it and Jake. She was prepared for this, ready to argue her case, but what would seeing him do to her confidence?

Struggling to forget about him and to concentrate on the task at hand, she skimmed her notes and reviewed her opening remarks. All she had to do was trick herself into believing this was a case like any other. Trick herself like she'd tricked herself into believing Jake cared for her. She forced the thought from her head. Tonight she could drown her regrets in ice cream. Right now she had a job to do.

The conference room door opened, and Sarah nearly jumped out of her seat. Everyone stood as Karen led in opposing counsel. Sarah's eyes quickly scanned the suited men, and her heart sank. Jake wasn't with them. Instead, Steve Manning and three younger attorneys filed in. Bonnie introduced Sarah and the arbitrator, and then Steve introduced his people. During the exchange, Sarah tried to catch

Steve's eye, to get some indication of what had happened to Jake, but he avoided her glance. Thankfully, Sarah wasn't the only one who noticed Jake's absence.

"Will Mr. Rappaport be joining us?" Bonnie asked.

Steve shook his head. "No, I'll be representing Lion Studios." His emotionless eyes met Sarah's. Clearly Jake's absence had something to do with her—something Steve obviously didn't appreciate.

Sarah struggled against her rising panic to keep her face emotionless. Had the Lion Studios bosses found out about their relationship? Had Jake been fired? Had he lied about what had happened and blamed her for trying to get information out of him? Did he plan to drag her down with him?

Sarah gripped her pen, waiting for Steve to announce their knowledge of a conflict of interest. She knew Lion Studios had the right to seek her removal from the case and order an investigation to determine if evidence had been compromised. Every aspect of her personal relationship with Jake would be divulged, not to mention her professional career ruined.

Steve leaned forward on the dark wood table, clasping his hands together in front of him, his face betraying nothing. Sarah gripped her pen so tightly, it dug into her hand.

"Shall we begin?" he asked, his voice calm and cool.

Sarah almost screamed in relief. He didn't say anything about her relationship with Jake. He didn't even indicate anything was wrong. Instead he acted as if everything was normal. Sarah stared at Steve in disbelief, relief washing over her.

"Sarah?" Bonnie prodded, indicating it was time for MAG

to start presenting its case. Sarah snapped out of her momentary shock and nervously spread her notes out on the table in front of her.

"Good morning, everyone," she began, quickly pulling her wandering thoughts back to the arbitration. Despite slightly stumbling over the first two sentences of her opening remarks, she quickly found her groove and flawlessly delivered her argument. In logical order she outlined her plan to prove MAG's case based on the terms of the Basic Agreement and the industry custom and practice governing payment of residuals for basic cable reruns. She briefly clarified the language of the residuals provision, then cited past instances where the language had successfully been applied and Lion Studios had correctly paid residuals.

When Sarah was finished, Steve presented his own opening remarks, asserting that the contract language was vague and unspecific. He outlined the studio's interpretation of the residuals provision and explained how Lion Studios believed the provision should be applied to this claim.

With the opening comments out of the way, the arbitration began in earnest. Each side presented its case, and the arbitrator listened intently, pausing every once in a while to push his glasses up the bridge of his nose. Each side called its expert witnesses, questioning and cross-examining them in a mild, almost boring way. Sarah chuckled a little to herself. Despite the glamour of the industry, one could hardly call this conference-room drama interesting.

Proceedings moved much more slowly than expected, and at noon the arbitrator called a recess for lunch. Lion Studios was shown to another conference room down the hall to enjoy their catered sandwiches and discuss strategy, while

Bonnie and Sarah ate their sandwiches in the conference room.

"You're doing great. If the afternoon session goes as well as the morning one, we'll have a victory for sure," Bonnie said, taking a sip of her diet soda.

"Thanks, but nothing is certain until we're done." Sarah nodded, appreciating the encouragement but not ready to celebrate yet. Despite the stressful excitement of the morning session, she was famished and quickly polished off a tuna sandwich. After she pushed the crumbs of her lunch aside, she and Bonnie spent the next half hour poring over their notes for the afternoon session.

With only ten minutes left for lunch, Sarah excused herself, hurrying out of the conference room and down the hall toward the ladies' room. She slowed her steps as she approached the Lion Studios conference room. Part of her hoped Steve might step out, giving her the chance to ask him about Jake. Disappointment quickly replaced hope when she walked down the empty hallway and the conference room door remained stubbornly shut. Silently she thanked her lucky stars. What was she doing, wishing for yet another risk? Hadn't she had enough near heart attacks in the last few weeks to last a lifetime? There would be time tomorrow to call Jake and find out what had happened. For now she had a job to do, and she was determined to do it.

The afternoon session proceeded as smoothly as the morning session, with the evidence from both sides presented at a slightly quicker pace. Finally, at nearly five o'clock, Sarah and Steve made their closing statements. The arbitrator nodded, promising to consider the evidence carefully before deciding and thanking everyone for coming.

Sarah leaned over to Bonnie, avoiding Steve's eye as he and the other Lion Studios lawyers collected their things. "How do you think we did?"

"I think we did well. Lion made some good arguments, but yours were better. However, we never know until we get the ruling."

They stood and shook hands with the other side before Karen came to escort Lion Studios back to the lobby.

"Thank you again for your services." Bonnie approached Allan and shook his hand.

"My pleasure." He smiled, pushing his glasses up with his other hand.

"When do you think we'll have your ruling?" Sarah asked, gathering up her papers.

Allan slid his notes and his copy of the evidence into a dark leather briefcase. "I make it a point to have an answer within two weeks. But, among the three of us, I'll say this much—you made the more convincing argument." He offered a knowing wink, and Sarah felt a huge weight lifted from her shoulders.

"I'll walk you out," Bonnie offered, but Allan shook his head.

"No need. I know the way. Have a great weekend, ladies." He waved, then left the room.

"Well done, Sarah," Bonnie congratulated. "I knew you'd come through for us."

"Thanks," Sarah replied, filled with a sense of confidence she hadn't felt in weeks. If only she was as confident about Jake. Now, with everything finally over, she had to know what had happened to him.

"Excuse me." She hurried to the conference room door.

"I forgot to ask Steve about one of the other Lion Studios claims."

"Call him Monday."

"No, I want to do it now before I forget. You know how it is."

Sarah hurried off down the corridor, reaching the lobby just as Steve stepped into the elevator with his co-workers.

"Steve," she called out, struggling to regain her composure as she hurried through the small lobby toward him. "I forgot to ask you about the *Hidden Pleasures* claim."

He shot her a puzzled look, placing his hand over the elevator door to stop it from closing. "The *Hidden Pleasures* claim? What claim?"

"The one Jake was working on," she said, hoping he'd understand.

He studied her for a second, then turned to his co-counsel. "I'll meet you guys downstairs." He stepped out of the elevator, allowing the doors to close behind him. Luckily, the doors to the other elevator immediately opened.

"Let's talk about it on the way down." He motioned her toward the waiting elevator, and they stepped inside. Standing next to him while the doors slid shut, Sarah wondered how she could ask him about Jake. Knowing a little something about Steve, she decided to be direct.

"What happened to Jake?" she asked.

He looked surprised. "You don't know?"

"I haven't talked to him. I thought he'd be here today."

"He quit yesterday."

"What?" Sarah asked, feeling as though the elevator had dropped seven stories in only a second.

"He's had enough of Lion Studios. Decided to join the family firm."

"The Virginia firm?" She didn't bother to hide the desperation in her question.

Before he could answer, the elevator came to a stop, and the doors slid open to reveal the rest of the Lion Studios attorneys waiting for Steve in the building's main lobby. He stepped out of the elevator, then turned around, offering her his hand. "Thank you for a rousing arbitration, Miss Steele."

"You're welcome," Sarah replied, doing to her best to shake hands with some semblance of professional courtesy.

"As for *Hidden Pleasures*, you should discuss it with Jake before it's too late," he added before walking off with his co-workers toward the parking structure.

Sarah tried not to gape at Steve as the elevator doors slid closed. She hit the button for the eighth floor, her mind reeling. How could Jake give up everything he'd worked so hard for? And what did Steve mean about talking to Jake? If she spoke to him, would it stop him from leaving? What would she say? What was there to say? Suddenly the answer was so clear and startling, she almost missed her floor when the elevator doors opened at the MAG lobby.

He loved her as much as she loved him, but he didn't know how she felt. She'd never told him, and she hadn't given him the chance to tell her. He'd proven his love by leaving Lion Studios when he could have continued with the case, knowing she wouldn't reveal their secret. Instead he'd quit, removing her from any professional danger. Wandering back to her office, she felt both elated and depressed. Elated because she finally knew how she felt and she wanted to tell Jake. Depressed because it might be too late.

"Are you all right?" Bonnie asked, watching Sarah amble back into the department.

Seeing her chance to get away, Sarah shook her head. "I don't think my sandwich agreed with me. Do you mind if I go home early?"

"Not at all. You deserve it. See you Monday."

Sarah grabbed her purse out of her office, careful not to hurry until she was out of the department. It took forever for the elevator to come; then, as if to deliberately frustrate her, it stopped on almost every floor, letting people on for the afternoon rush home. She sprinted out of the elevator once it reached the main lobby, cursing the heels she'd worn for the arbitration. Kicking them off, she picked them up and hurried to the parking garage, her nylons shredding on the rough concrete floor. Pulling open her car door, she tossed everything into the passenger seat, hopped in, started the engine, and sped out of the garage.

Getting to Santa Monica this late on a Friday was a nightmare. The surface streets were clogged, and the early sunset didn't improve anyone's driving. As she sat in traffic, she dug through her purse, looking for her cell phone. The image of it sitting in the charger on her desk came to mind. It was too late to go back for it. If Jake wasn't at his place, she'd wait outside his door until he came back—anything, if it meant seeing him and working everything out.

What if he won't see me? Sarah worried as she inched her car along in traffic, hoping to make it through the intersection on the next green light. What if she got there only to find out his quitting had nothing to do with her? Perhaps, like David, he'd never truly cared for her. No, that wasn't the case. She'd always had doubts about David, but she'd chosen to ignore them, believing she was somehow to blame for those feelings. She'd even ignored his dishonesty, believing his lame excuses though in the back of her mind she'd known the truth. Jake never gave her such doubts and worries. If nothing else, she always felt he was honest with her, even when she wasn't honest with him.

If he was so honest, then why hadn't he called her? Why hadn't he told her he'd quit Lion Studios? The questions popped into her head, but she ignored them. She'd hardly been open to conversation with him at El Amigo, so she couldn't blame him for not calling her.

Stepping on the gas pedal, she sped through the intersection just as the light was changing from yellow to red. Up ahead, the freeway was surprisingly clear due to an accident blocking the left two lanes a few miles back. Taking advantage of the open road, she sped toward Santa Monica, watching the sun continue to drop toward the horizon.

Getting through Santa Monica was another headache, and she didn't reach Jake's building until almost six o'clock. Luckily, she found parking on the street in front of his building. After throwing a few quarters into the meter, she dashed through the lobby toward the elevator, offering a quick wave to the doorman. It took only a minute to reach his floor, and when the elevator doors opened, she hurried down the hall toward Jake's.

Taking a deep breath, she raised a shaking hand and pushed the doorbell. She heard it buzz deep inside the condo. If he was home, what would she say to him? It didn't matter. She'd think of something, anything, to keep him from leaving and to make him realize how much she loved him.

As she shifted from foot to foot, her stomach tightened

at the sound of footsteps on the other side of the door. Her heart quickened, practically jumping out of her throat until the door opened, nearly bringing it to a stop.

"Hi, can I help you?" A tall, blond, very attractive woman greeted her with a smile.

Sarah nearly choked on her words, using every ounce of her strength to remain standing. She glanced over the woman's shoulder at a number of boxes spread around the room. On the coffee table two drink glasses and the remains of takeout sat next to a mountain of blue legal files. Sarah tried to take everything in but couldn't. Instead she examined the woman standing before her. Slim, attractive, and dressed in a designer suit that hugged her curves and accentuated her hips, the woman oozed elegance. All Sarah could do was stand there in her shredded nylons and stare. There was no sign of Jake, and whatever was going on between him and this woman, Sarah didn't want to know.

"Can I help you?" the woman asked again, snapping Sarah out of her stupor.

"I must have knocked on the wrong door," Sarah forced through a weak smile. "Sorry for disturbing you."

She bolted back down the hall toward the elevator, wiping her cheeks with the back of one hand, struggling to make sense of the torrent of emotions screaming for attention.

Chapter Eleven

Y ou're jumping to conclusions," Dinah said, standing in front of Sarah.

"So?" Sarah replied, pulling the blanket tighter around her shoulders. She'd spent the whole day on the couch in her pajamas, swimming in a lake of self-indulgent remorse. She didn't appreciate Dinah's coming home and horning in on her pity-party.

"Has he called?" she pointed out. Despite leaving her cell phone at work, she'd checked her voice mail enough times to know he hadn't.

"Have you called? It isn't 1950. You could pick up the phone," Dinah retorted.

"Do you always have to be so blunt?"

"Apparently so."

Sarah frowned. "You're blocking the TV."

Dinah switched off the TV, then snatched the cordless phone off its receiver, holding it out to Sarah. "Call him."

"Why? So I can find out the truth? I know what I saw: an attractive woman, drinks, takeout. What else could it be?"

Tears stung the corners of her eyes, but she fought them back. She was out of tissues and tired of wiping her face on the blanket.

"If you call him, you'll find out."

"If I don't call him, I might get through this holiday season with some shred of my dignity left." Sarah picked up the remote, leaning around Dinah to click the TV back on. "Besides, Steve already said he's going back to Virginia."

Undaunted, Dinah sat down in the chair next to the sofa and continued to stare at Sarah. Sarah tried to ignore her, but Dinah just kept staring.

"What?" Sarah snapped, a little ashamed of herself for acting so childishly.

"You're being ridiculous," Dinah said gently, making Sarah feel more foolish than before. She clicked off the TV and tossed the remote onto the coffee table.

"I know. And I know I'm probably jumping to conclusions, but I can't take another heartbreak. Not after David."

"You need to forget David. You might even want to thank him."

"Thank him?"

"Yeah, for helping you move on, get a better job, meet new people. He didn't ruin your life, Sarah—he only dented it a bit. Now it's up to you to take advantage of your freedom."

"And call a serial womanizer with no interest in me?"

A smirk pulled at the corners of Dinah's mouth. "At the very least, regular dinner dates at Sushi Catalina would be nice."

Sarah tossed a small pillow at her friend, smiling in spite of herself. "Yeah, it beats most of my dinners."

"Then what have you got to lose?"

My heart, my mind, my belief in true love, Sarah thought but didn't say it. Dinah was right. There was no point moping. So Jake didn't love her. Eventually she would have had a rebound relationship; what did it matter if it was with Jake? Because he was more than a rebound, and she knew it. She'd allowed herself to fall in love, putting herself and her career in jeopardy, and look how it had ended. It hadn't even ended. It had simply fizzled.

"Look, the Lion Studios Christmas party is tonight, and for the second year in a row, I don't have a date," Dinah continued. "Come with me. Maybe there's some other exec you could date. One not in Labor Relations."

"Ha-ha, very funny," Sarah said, not appreciating Dinah's attempt at humor.

"I'm serious, at least about the coming-with-me part."

"Did Jake call and put you up to this?"

Dinah threw up her hands in self-defense. "No, not this time."

Sarah leaned back against the couch, wanting to pull the blanket over her head and hide. "What if he's there?"

"What if he is?"

The question hit Sarah like a bucket of ice water. What was she so afraid of? She'd faced bigger heartache and disappointment than Jake Rappaport. Besides, what were the chances he'd attend? He was probably busy packing for Virginia or making love to his leggy blond friend.

Well, let him, she thought, tossing aside her blanket. "You're right. What if he is? I just won one of the biggest arbitrations of my life. Why should I let another man in the arms of another blond make me feel bad about myself?"

"I totally agree."

Sarah stood with a new sense of determination. "Let him show up. Let him bring his new fling. Screw Jake. I'm going out tonight and celebrating."

Dinah jumped to her feet, clapping. "Now, that's the Sarah I know."

Two hours later, Sarah followed Dinah through the false-storefront sets toward the large party tent in the center of the Lion Studios lot. The familiar strains of Christmas carols spilled out of the tent, along with employees in various states of revelry. Some stood around chatting, while others wandered through the fake forests of Christmas trees flanking the tent. A snow machine attached to the top of a crane provided a gentle dusting of white, while numerous spotlights at the base of the tent illuminated the gently descending flakes.

Wearing an evening dress of deep blue covered by a small jacket, her hair carefully arranged in an elegant but simple twist, Sarah felt, strangely, more confident than she had three weeks ago when Jake escorted her through these same false streets. A few worries still bothered her. How would he react if she saw him tonight? Would he ignore her? Would he chat with her like David did the last time they spoke, each word laced with sarcasm and thinly veiled contempt?

So what if he does? she thought. She was no high school girl but a woman, a lawyer, someone who could stand up to anything.

She followed Dinah though the fake igloo entrance into the tent. The interior was decorated like a winter wonderland, the tent seams lined with strands of white lights hung with sparkling crystal snowflakes. In the center stood a large tree decorated with white birds, silver snowflakes, gilded ribbon, and tinsel. Faux snow drifted slowly down from machines rigged up in the corners, giving the party a magical, surreal feel.

"It's beautiful," Sarah said, taking it all in.

"Yeah, Lion Studios goes all out for this."

Several hundred people mingled, some eating, others dancing on a wooden platform at the far end near the DJ. Most people stood around chatting and laughing, enjoying the hosted bar and the seasonal atmosphere. Sarah's eyes scanned the crowd, but in the semidarkness she could barely make out individuals. She caught herself, realizing there was only one face she was looking for. Even if he was here, what were the chances she'd see him?

"Oh, there's Christine—she works with me," Dinah said. "You have to meet her. You'll love her." Dinah headed off across the tent. Sarah started to follow, but a group of laughing, suited men stepped in front of her, cutting her off. She pushed past them, craning her head in an effort to spot Dinah in the crowd. Standing on tiptoe, she cursed her diminutive height, wishing she'd worn higher heels instead of her lower, more comfortable ones. Dinah was nowhere to be seen. Sarah reached into her purse to pull out her cell phone and call Dinah, then softly cursed under her breath, remembering that the phone was still sitting in the charger in her office.

Suddenly, a small gap in the crowd opened, offering a perfect view of the Christmas tree—and Jake standing underneath it chatting with Steve Manning and the blond from his condo. Sarah's fingers froze over the purse's zipper as Jake turned, his eyes locking with hers.

All she wanted to do was run to him, throw her arms around his neck, and kiss him in a way to make him never forget her. Instead she stood still, her heartbeat pounding in her ears. He continued to stare at her with a look she couldn't read. Did he hate her for destroying his career? Did he blame her for forcing him to leave Lion Studios? Embarrassment washed over her while she struggled to read his features in the dim light.

Beating the feeling down, she remembered her pledge to not let a man ruin the evening. Drawing herself up, she offered Jake a sarcastic little wave before turning on her heel and making a beeline toward the back of the tent. She might refuse to let him ruin the evening, but she wasn't about to stand there and let him make a fool out of her either.

Hurrying though an opening in the tent, she found herself at the back of the fake forest, the trees twinkling with hundreds of white LED lights, their branches covered in a dusting of man-made snow. There was no one about. Most people were still inside, keeping warm at the bar or on the dance floor. A few people milled about the forest entrance, but Sarah, having slipped in through the back, stood unnoticed. She took a deep breath of the refreshingly cold air, thankful to be out of the hot confines of the crowded tent. Holding out a hand, she caught a few snowflakes, watching them melt into little drops of water on her palm. She closed her eyes, the crisp scent of the pine trees soothing her, and for a moment she imagined herself back home, enjoying the first light dusting of winter snow.

Opening her eyes, she pulled her jacket tighter, watching her breath rise in little clouds to join the snow.

"It's beautiful," she said aloud to herself, rubbing her arms for warmth.

"Yes, you are."

She whirled around to see Jake standing behind her, the open tent flap rustling in the breeze. Cautious hope rose up in her heart. He'd followed her. He wanted to talk to her, though probably to chew her out for the damage she'd done to his career. However, his handsome face, made softer by the LED lights, held no trace of anger. Instead he seemed cautious, approaching her as though she was going to run away again. There was no running away this time. She'd face him as she'd faced David, no matter what the outcome.

"I thought you quit," she said, struggling to stop shivering.

He stepped closer, not shrinking under the defiant look she shot him. "I did."

"Then why are you here?" Sarah didn't step back as he moved closer, his breath rising in the air to meet hers.

"To see you."

He swept her into a deep embrace, his lips enveloping hers. Her eyes went wide with shock before her body surrendered to the need in his touch, the tenderness, yearning, and longing in his kiss. She fell into his chest, reveling in the taste and feel of him, in his warm hands on her back, his slightly rough cheek beneath her fingers. Hope flared in her before the icy fingers of jealousy took hold.

She broke free of his kiss, attempting to step away, but he held her tightly.

"You won't get away from me so easily this time," he

whispered with the sly grin she'd come to love over the last three weeks.

"What about her?" Sarah asked, resisting the delicious feel of his warm arms around her.

He shot her a puzzled look. "Who?"

"The woman I saw in your condo yesterday."

Jake thought for a moment, then threw back his head and laughed. "You mean Lisa? Lisa Williams? She's one of the attorneys in my family's firm. The case she's handling was moved to California, and she doesn't want to stay here. My father wants to start a West Coast office, so she came here to bring me up to speed on the case. She's going home Monday, to her husband and two kids."

Relief softened Sarah's tense shoulders, and she fell into Jake's embrace. "You're not moving to Virginia?"

"No. Not unless you want to come with me."

He bent to kiss her, but she placed her palms flat against his chest to stop him. Despite the excitement of the moment, questions remained to be answered.

"So you still want to cross-examine me?" he asked.

"You have a number of outstanding charges."

"Ask me anything," he replied, kissing her lightly on the forehead, almost making her forget her questions.

"You're under oath to answer truthfully," she whispered as he nuzzled her neck, his warm lips teasing her cold skin.

"I swear to tell the truth." He kissed one cheek.

"The whole truth." He kissed the other cheek.

"And nothing but the truth." His lips gently brushed hers. "Now, what do you want to know?"

Pulling back from the dizzying kiss, Sarah watched the

snow settle on his hair. For a moment she thought of abandoning her questions along with all her doubts and throwing herself on the mercy of trust. However, there were things she had to know.

"Did you ask me out because you had feelings for me or because of the claim?" she asked.

His fingers whispered across her cheek as he pushed a loose strand of hair behind her ear. "You might have forgotten me after law school, but I never forgot you. It came back to me the day we had lunch. The more we spoke and the more I got to know you, the more I realized I couldn't let someone as special as you get away from me a second time."

She grasped his hand where it lingered near her neck, burying her cheek in the strong warmth of it. Tears threatened at the corners of her eyes, his words touching her in a way no man had ever touched her before. She placed her hands on either side of his face, feeling the rough stubble on his cheeks. "Why didn't you tell me you'd quit? Why did you let me go into the arbitration thinking you'd be there?"

Jake chuckled. "You wouldn't let me tell you. I also knew you needed the space to work, without distractions or interference. Judging from what Steve told me, you did."

"I won."

"I knew you would."

"You're saying Steve compromised the case?" she teased.

"Not at all. You're the better lawyer."

Sarah pulled him down to her, kissing him with a passion she'd never felt before. He met her passion, clinging to her, crushing her as if he'd never let her go.

"I love you, Sarah," he whispered, nibbling her earlobe.

"I love you too."

Closing her eyes, she allowed her tears to spill out. He kissed them away, his lips brushing against one cheek, then the other before enveloping her mouth in a sweet, tender kiss.

WITHDRAWN